THE JEWEL OF LIFE

For the children of Goshen,
with abiding friendship.

Anna Kirwan Vogel

THE JEWEL OF LIFE

ANNA KIRWAN-VOGEL

ILLUSTRATED BY
DAVID WILGUS

Jane Yolen Books
Harcourt Brace Jovanovich, Publishers
SAN DIEGO NEW YORK LONDON

HBJ

Library of Congress Cataloging-in-Publication Data
Kirwan-Vogel, Anna.
The jewel of life / by Anna Kirwan-Vogel.—1st ed.
p. cm.
"Jane Yolen books."
Summary: Duffy, young apprentice to the alchemist Master Crowe, finds within himself an unsuspected natural magic that opens doorways into other worlds but also endangers their household.
ISBN 0-15-200750-4
[1. Fantasy.] I. Title.
PZ7.K6396Je 1991
[Fic]—dc20 90-36818

Designed by Michael Farmer
Printed in the United States of America
First edition
A B C D E

This book was begun for James Kief, Ian, Jessakye, Eowyn, Phoedre, and Greg, and completed for Korena, Max, and Robin.

Thank you, Sister Alberta,
for telling me I could write.

—A.K.-V.

Contents

Concerning Use of This Book

It is a curious fact: Magic does not go in a straight line. From beginning to end, its going is more like a circle, and the beginning for you *is anywhere you happen to enter. Wherever you are at this moment, you are near a doorway into the most profound mysteries of the infinite worlds of wonder.*

The keys to such doors are often words. Which of the words open which doors? Examples, clues, and hints are given throughout this primer, but the apprentice must look up and perform any given spell with a minimum of assistance and a maximum of tidiness, if it is to work at full strength.

CHAPTER 1

A SMALL APPRENTICE

IS NAME IS DUFFY," SAID MASTER HUMphrey, the almshouse beadle.

"Given name or family?" the apothecary wanted to know.

"Only name we know of. No family to bother you. He's a fine eleven years old, Master Crowe."

"Then they were short, lean years with scant growing seasons," Crowe answered dryly. He guessed the boy was nine, and his guess was close.

The boy called Duffy looked at his feet. He was used to being easily dismissed. But this might be the last master to come a-hiring. Duffy looked up again.

"No, no, this boy's been here so long, his page is filled in the ledger of charges against the Lord Mayor's Fund," Master Humphrey insisted. "He's old enough to be stubborn, unfortunately, but he knows the size of switch that is his better. He's bright, he is. He'll learn to serve well enough."

It was the third day of the late summer Poke Fair. The last of the year's harvest hiring was being done, and the last crop of apprentices were being signed onto the guild lists, their keep paid out to the merchants who would train, feed, and house them until they could pay their own way. Master Humphrey had herded all the orphans, foundlings, paupers, and simpletons kept at the almshouse into a rope-ringed booth at the edge of the market, near the guildhall of Elford Town. They stood now in a ragged row, smallest to tallest. Almost cheerless, not quite homeless, they furtively or artlessly scratched their itches. They chewed their dirty nails. The big ones bumped against the small ones and took over their standing room. The smaller ones staggered to keep their balance and shifted ground. On the whole, they looked cowed and disorderly.

For three days, idle townsfolk had looked on while prospective mistresses and masters inspected and estimated the meager worth of the untaught youngsters. The pick of the litter were long gone.

"No livery to go with this one," one loutish pauper muttered rudely for the smaller boys to hear.

"What does that mean?" asked an orphan named Hugh Defoe.

"That's Crowe, the ditch-picker," the tall lout, George Tallow, growled under his breath. "That old bird says his herbs chase rats as well as my stoat does. Stole a threepenny scullery hunt from me, he did." He spit on a grassless patch of dirt. "Don't he make your flesh creep? People say he does black magic, too," he added. "They say he has powers."

Duffy tried to hear everything George said about Master Crowe, without missing what Master Humphrey was saying about Duffy's page in the accounts. He heard George say "stoat," though, and "flesh," and "black magic."

"Do you want him to hire you?" Hugh asked George doubtfully.

"That old quack-grass grubber?" George scoffed. He said it rather loudly, and Master Humphrey swiveled to glare at him. When the beadle had turned back to the apothecary, George went on. "See this arm?" he boasted, flexing it for emphasis. "I will let you know which trade I choose—when the better merchants and captains come to see who's likely. And I'll pick something that feeds a fellow better and gives more chances to get close to things I want than that old devil ever would."

"Let's have a look, lad," the apothecary Crowe was saying meanwhile to Duffy.

He had really hoped to take an older child into his service, for his work was difficult, and sometimes it was decidedly peculiar. But he was an old man, and poor, and could not be choosy. He knew that all the clever boys of twelve and fourteen wished to be the apprentices of fencing masters and pastry cooks. They thought it dull to climb ladders and fetch dusty vials of *vinum citrinum* or pots of powdered willow bark or horehound or other remedies. They thought it would be duller still to dress in plain jerkins and learn to read and write, when they might have been learning to ride and fight, or to construct fairy palaces of almond paste and spun sugar. It seemed he had little choice in the matter.

He looked the rest of the ragged crew over, about a dozen of them, all told: boys with no shoes, girls with hair like rats' nests. Duffy looked pretty much like the rest. Master Crowe was not sure what to think. A less likely-looking apprentice would have been hard to find, even among this lot. He turned back, and peered at Duffy almost as if he were buying a horse.

"Hair blond—tangled and untrimmed," he mused aloud. "The face is honest, if a trifle wary. What's this across the nose? A tuppence worth of freckles, no more. The features are pleasant, I would say. Skin clear of pockmarks. Surprisingly well scrubbed. Hmm."

Duffy heard only some of Crowe's quiet inventory. What he heard was, "*Face . . . nose? A tuppence worth . . . freckles . . . pockmarks. . . .*" Not only was he used to being dismissed, he was also used to being insulted, but he didn't like being talked about in such humiliating detail. He squirmed.

"And eyes . . . ," Master Crowe continued the mumbled

evaluation. There was no denying the boy had remarkable eyes, for they were alert and inquisitive, and green-gold as the sun-flecked river that ran through Elford.

But the youngster looked underfed, "And might well be, considering the reputation of almshouse dinners." The apothecary spoke out loud suddenly, startling Duffy into a half smile which Crowe half saw. The old man was thinking that the jerkin, at any rate, was too large, probably a hand-down from some other pauper. It was certainly worn enough to have belonged to half a dozen boys. The shirt and hose that went with it were nearly threadbare, and so faded as to have no distinguishable color at all.

"Lean as a January squirrel and ragged as a tomcat's ears," Master Crowe remarked to the beadle.

Duffy stared at the floor, avoiding Master Humphrey's critical eye. If the old man didn't like him, why did he not just go over to the other boys and pick someone he liked better? Bertie was taller, and no one could say Hugh was thin. George Tallow, for that matter, was the strong one. He was the best dressed, too, as he'd stolen a white shirt from among laundry drying on somebody's hedge. *If size and style are the things this old man goes by,* Duffy wished, *let him move along.* Master Humphrey would grow angry if this went on much longer.

Crowe noticed the boy's gaze and the unchildlike stiffness of his body. He had remarked the beadle's comment about switches, and he guessed there might be fresh welts across Duffy's skinny back. Crowe shook his grey head ruefully. Perhaps this one was a troublemaker. But what could such a sorry stick of a boy have done to deserve a beating? Of course, he might simply have slept ill on a hard floor.

Crowe eyed the beadle for a moment, then turned his attention back to Duffy. *What is it about him, in particular, that is likable? Sore or not,* he realized, *at least the boy stands straight and doesn't skulk or slouch as some might.*

"What do you know about apothecary shops?" Crowe asked abruptly.

"A . . . about apothecary . . . nothing, sir. By your leave, sir. I mean, there's herbs and tonics and such, I suppose, for fevers and all. . . ." Duffy's words petered out and he fell silent again.

"Bittersweet and camomile salve," Crowe muttered, then shut his mouth. The salve was good for bruises. He was mildly amazed to find his mind made up of itself. He would take on this Duffy as an apprentice, young though he might be.

Bertie Trewes, an orphan just a bit lankier and sootier than Duffy, whispered, "Tell him . . . uh . . . tell him it's where you get, you know, wormwood. And garlic knots." Bertie talked out of the corner of his mouth. He did not wish to attract the Masters' eyes, and his advice fell almost invisibly down to Duffy's ears.

But Crowe, by this time, was reading a parchment the beadle had all ready for his signature. "Two shillings for his upkeep?" he chided irritably. "You'll give me no less than ten. I intend to feed him sufficient."

" 'Black magic,' says George," Bertie whispered. "If Crowe can get more money out of old Fatty-Sit-on-the-Coinbox, I'll believe it's black magic. Ooh, lookie here, they're going to get the ink. *Some*one's going to be pulling up ditch-root with the old man."

Duffy hardly listened to the dealing of the apothecary and the beadle, for all that they were buying and selling years of his own life. Just then, it made little difference to him what manner of master he got, so long as he need not stay another day with Master Humphrey.

He straightened, and his back ached again. He had indeed been beaten recently—not once, but twice, when he had not intentionally done wrong—and now he was sullen and silent, as well as sore. He was not old enough to comprehend all the strange things said in Elford about Crowe, but he was quite old enough to know the Elford almshouse would always mean more beatings. He kept his mouth shut, tried not to fidget, and was all in all rather relieved to see the old man sign the apprenticeship papers.

Master Crowe blotted the last ink off his quill with the beadle's smudgy pen-wiper. He had not driven the bargain all the way home, because he'd become impatient to be gone. Catching Duffy's eye, Crowe remarked, "That's that, then. You're my helper, Duffy, and may our work prosper."

CHAPTER 2

THE SIGN OF THE MANDRAKE AND MARJORAM

UST WHERE BREAD-AND-CHEESE STREET veered toward the Meadows Gate, a wet path called Tea Steep Alley cut down to the riverbank. Duffy had never noticed the apothecary shop wedged into the huddle of shutter-fronted houses. Their main doors were at street level. Their back doors were a story or so below, on the alley. To one side was a brewer's shop; on the other side, a glove-perfumer. The wooden sign above the apothecary's lintel did not hang out over the street. Perhaps, Duffy thought, that was why he hadn't remarked it before. Now that he really looked at it, he saw it was a painting of a pointy-toed man all made of roots, and a bundle of green twigs.

"The house at the sign of the Mandrake and Marjoram," Crowe informed Duffy.

Like most of the small merchants' booths in Elford, Crowe's herb shop had a large set of shuttered, unglazed windows. It also had, Duffy saw, a brass keyhole-plate shaped like a gaping watchdog. The keyhole was the dog's mouth.

"Mandrake for headache, marjoram for a cold stomach. Roots and berries and leaves, Duffy." He sighed. "Much to do."

" 'Mandrake for headache,' " Duffy murmured.

Crowe threw him a sharp glance, then pulled a big key out of a pocket inside his sleeve, and unlocked the door. Pushing it open, he waved Duffy ahead of him into the stuffy, fragrant shop.

Duffy blinked. He was impatient for his eyes to adjust to the shadowy room. The only dim light leaked down a stairwell from some upper-story window. Crowe was already lifting the bars that held the street shutters closed, but he didn't open them just yet.

Duffy began to see that the shop was lined with simple wooden shelves, bins, and cupboards, and hanging bunches of leaves and pods. Pushing aside a rust-colored baize curtain in the far corner of the shop, Crowe heaved open the door it had concealed. Duffy hoped there was a kitchen below stairs. He followed Crowe willingly down a rickety pile of steps that would have pinched the shoulders of, or pitched headlong, a man one whit less slight and crumpled than his new master. The steps became a corridor that burrowed along for a while and then, quite suddenly, twisted itself into a cavernous cellar. It was not a kitchen, and Duffy's stomach growled once in mild protest.

"Sit yourself down, boy," the apothecary said, his voice firm and kindly.

Duffy, who could think of no reply, simply climbed onto a tall three-legged stool and, catlike, occupied himself with a thorough examination of his surroundings.

It was an unusual cellar. For one thing, there were chunks of machinery here and there on the shelves, like great, dark fragments of clockwork. Some were enclosed in blown glass: caught and bottled, as if they'd been dragonflies. There were two large braziers in which the dead coals and ashes still shimmered with mute color; the flames that had leapt there might have burned rainbows. A dwarf skeleton hung from a bronze rod embedded in the wall. The skeleton had arms that dangled to its knees, and fingers too short for the hands that splayed them. And crouched among the remedies and simples and bunches of drying herbs were stuffed and dusty birds and filmy-eyed reptiles floating in bottles of amber liquor.

It was a room brimming with unforgettable objects he could not name or place, and Duffy's shoulders hunched up in a sudden, dreamlike chill. He did not imagine he would ever be comfortable in that cellar, and he held onto the sides of his stool as if he expected to be tumbled off at any moment.

It had not occurred to Crowe beforehand what his cobwebbed workshop would look like to a boy. Now, though, one glance at Duffy's worried posture caused him to look around afresh at the shelves. Even to his own eyes, it was not a usual sort of place.

Master Crowe smiled to himself. He understood how much courage and ease may have to do with cheerful noise and a full stomach, so he puttered and rattled about, producing a lump of black bread, apples, and two mugs of thin, bluish milk. Somehow, their appearance from such sinister-looking shelves was reassuring to Duffy.

"Not that you'll always eat such dainties," Crowe muttered wryly to him, "but Mistress Cotter has finally paid for the wart cure I gave her in March." Since Duffy seemed to be attending, he went on. "And a hard time I had, convincing her it was right that she should pay. The cure I gave her, alas, was sovereign for warts, but not for mismade chins. I could not bottle up a miracle for her, and she was not satisfied with what I could do."

Duffy nodded over his dinner. He knew Mistress Cotter. "She is a foul old thing," he ventured at last. "Master Humphrey showed George Tallow and me to her, for she wished to take on a page, to make her neighbors think her fine. She is thinking of taking on George for a yard boy—he's too big for a page—but she would not have *me* at all."

Master Crowe was clearly interested in this conversation, and, thus encouraged, Duffy went on. "She fancies now she wants instead a pretty spaniel, to put a ribbon around its neck and call it baby names. But if you ask me, a spaniel would probably bite her as soon as look at her." All of a sudden, Duffy stopped speaking and looked somewhat alarmed at how freely his tongue had been running along.

"You did not please Mistress Cotter?" the old man asked. "Why, what happened?"

Duffy stared at a bunch of dry leaves hanging from a rafter. After a moment he said, "I sneezed on her, is all."

"That was not respectful nor courteous, when she thought to give you a place."

"Indeed I know, sir," Duffy answered miserably. "I did not mean to do it. But she made me stand with my hands behind my back, and then she wished to see my teeth, and her hand was covered with flour or some such powder to make it white and fine, and she held it under my nose. One cannot stop some sneezes, sir, and my mouth did spray, by itself. She said I was bad luck and made me stand aside. But it was not my fault."

"I have misjudged your virtue," Master Crowe apologized graciously. "Truly, one cannot stop some sneezes." Then with a canny grin he added, "And I think, anyway, that you would not have looked well with a ribbon around your neck, trotting at Mistress Cotter's heels down Market Road. You are more suitable to apprenticeship than to petting."

Duffy's jaw fairly dropped at that. Was he not to be punished for his wickedness? The blunt fact was, courtesy and justice were such strangers, he scarcely recognized them. But opportunity—now, that was a different matter. And it occurred to Duffy suddenly that he might very soon have a chance to finish well a certain scheme he'd begun badly.

It was not much later that Crowe showed Duffy the straw pallet in the back of the cellar where he was to sleep, and, taking the only candle with him, went off to bed himself. As soon as he was reasonably certain the old man was asleep, Duffy crept out the back gate of the shop and disappeared up the alley, heading toward the almshouse.

The night air was cool and the alley dark, and Duffy concentrated on making no sound, putting one foot stealthily in front of the other. He did not look up toward the narrow loft window that hung out over the shadowed mews, so he did not know that Crowe, gazing at the stars as he did every clear night, heard a noise below him and saw his new apprentice leaving.

"Running away?" Crowe asked aloud. He had not imagined the boy would be homesick for his former life, and Duffy had not mentioned any mates he would miss. "What, then? Should I fetch after, follow him, and bring him back?"

Crowe knew apprentices often ran away. But he had not counted on this sort of trouble. He had liked the boy, had thought the arrangement was satisfactory all around—except that the boy was young.

He was still ruminating at the window a few minutes later when Duffy reappeared, clutching some awkward sort of bundle. The boy hurried along to the shop, and the old man heard the latch rattle.

By the time the apothecary had descended the two flights of stairs, Duffy was huddled on his pallet. He did not pretend to be asleep, though, and looked up warily when Crowe's candlelight wavered into the cellar. That pleased Crowe, and he changed his mind about mentioning what he'd seen. Instead he asked brusquely, "Did Master Humphrey beat you much on missing that page position? I meant to tell you, there's salve here for bruises. Also for flea bites. You'll sleep more comfortably if you use it."

The light of the candle was faint and golden. Duffy saw Crowe's face hovering in the surrounding darkness and felt a chill that was neither cold nor fear. But when the apothecary brought out a pot of herb cream for his welted back, he began for the first time to understand his good fortune at finding such a master.

Quickly he tugged off his shirt. The old man's sure fingers touched the sore back gently but with authority, smoothing the salve into the wounds. Duffy waited for Master Crowe to make some mention of the stripes he found, but when the apothecary continued to work without comment, Duffy relaxed. For a moment he thought guiltily of his secret errand, but then he put the thought aside.

Master Crowe returned the salve to its shelf and came back with a red-lacquered tin spice box.

"Sometimes a simple sweet at bedtime cures sore dreams," he remarked. "Would you like to chew on an anise twig? It will leave a pleasant flavor in your mouth."

It was the first time anyone had ever offered him "a simple sweet." The anise tasted tingly and mysterious. And as he began to drift toward sleep, all that was grateful and loyal in Duffy's thin frame rallied. He would not have given up service with Master Crowe for all the pastry cooks and fencing instructors in Elford Town.

CHAPTER 3

MASTER CROWE'S OTHER WORK

HERE WAS GREY LIGHT LEAKING IN AROUND the door of the back passageway. Duffy pushed away his blanket and tiptoed over to the stairs. No sound came from above. Master Crowe did not seem to be about yet. Duffy was aware of a faint fustiness. The cellar itself was curious, but that smell—of herbs and must, damp stone and mice, and the slightest trace of cinnamon and clove—that smell was actually far more affecting. It was not unpleasant, but it was pervasive. New and foreign, it stirred him; and yet, it made him feel, too, as if he were about to remember something.

"Have I been dreaming?" he whispered aloud, then shook his head. He wasn't sure.

In the corner farthest from the staircase was a pile of refuse. There, half-covered by rags, was the pierced tin box that Duffy had tucked underneath for safety. As apprentice, he was bound to be the one to tend the rubbish. He had hopes his secret would go undiscovered for some time.

The two eggs he had eased out of the coop at the far end of the alley were also there under the rags.

"Stewbone," Duffy whispered, prying up the lid of the box, "here is your breakfast."

The animal hissed when Duffy poked the eggs into the box. Her buff-colored fur bristled, and her black eyes never wavered or glanced away from him. She ignored the eggs.

"It's all right," he said. "I won't let George get you again. Him and his stoat-running! I'll take proper care of you." Gingerly, Duffy put one hand toward the beast, but she hissed again, and the sight of her teeth caused him to withdraw it hastily. "It's all right," he repeated soothingly. "You just eat now, Stewbone."

The stoat was still watching him warily. Duffy thought he had never seen anything as black and bright as her eyes.

"*Stewbone* is an ugly name," he decided. "I won't call you that just because George did." Duffy tried to think of another name, one that sounded sweet and noble and friendly. "I will call you Iseult," he said finally.

Just then there was a noise upstairs. Duffy quickly pulled a few rags back over the tin box, and ran across the room to the fireplace. When Master Crowe came in, his new apprentice was already busy stirring the coals.

"Good, good, child," the old man approved. Then he showed Duffy how to boil the kettle to make thin porridge for their morning meal.

Afterwards, when the dishes had been cleared away and scoured, Crowe bid Duffy fetch a load of charcoal.

"For I intend," he explained, "to show you some wondrous sights that will make you start with amazement."

He smiled when he said it, and Duffy thought that must be his master's notion of a little jest. He could not imagine what would be so amazing about watching Master Crowe mix remedies for the stomachache and vapors, but he was reluctant to say so. Besides, the charcoal was near the pile of rubbish where Iseult was hidden, and he didn't want the old man's attention drawn in that direction for any reason. So he brought the charcoal and heaped it in a brazier as he was directed.

Meanwhile, Crowe was setting up bits of apparatus, pulling pans from one shelf and strangely shaped dishes from another. As he flapped about in his tattered robe and skullcap, he did resemble a large blackbird.

Duffy watched him from an ever-growing pool of questions. *How old was Master Crowe?* Fifty hard years might bow a man's back and blanch his hair until it was ashen as the apothecary's. *On the other hand,* Duffy thought, *anyone with knowledge of herbs and unguents might be expected to fend off wrinkles for many years.*

Yet Crowe's grey eyes peered out of a venerable web of lines and creases. They were honest wrinkles, too, not greasy folds like the ones that outlined Master Humphrey's fat jowls. And old, older, or ancient, the apothecary was spry as a boy, hustling back and forth connecting and balancing pieces of equipment. When Crowe was done, the worktable was covered from end to end. Duffy himself could not have been any quicker.

Over the charcoal-brazier stood a metal tripod on which sat an egg-shaped little jug of hard, glazed pottery. Balanced atop the neck of the jug was a cap with a long, long beak extending far to the side, through a hole in one rim of a shallow pan and out again at the opposite edge. Under the spout of this long-nosed jug, where it might catch drips, was an iron pot.

Now the apothecary lifted a stone slab from the floor and showed Duffy a dark, damp stone cistern in the earth, and the mossy bucket that hung there.

"Water," he said, before emptying the cold water into the middle pan of his arrangement, so that it covered the pottery spout.

Finally, he brought out a skin bag of some dark liquid and poured it into the jug over the fire Duffy had just kindled in the brazier.

Ah, thought Duffy, *that is some potion he will cook up to cure folks.* But when he sniffed at the leather bottle, he found it was nothing but wine. Was all this elaborate activity merely for the sake of a cupful of warm wine? Duffy thought it would be rude to ask such an impertinent question, especially since Master Crowe seemed as intent on the boiling as if he had been melting gold.

At the end of the spout, drops began to fall into the iron pot. In the dim cellar light, they shimmered like dew, all the dark ruby color of the wine rinsed away.

"There, tell me what you see now, my boy," said Master Crowe.

Duffy flushed with embarrassment and stammered, "I see that you have changed wine into water, sir, and I doubt not it is a great art, but . . ." He thought perhaps he ought to hold his tongue then, for he did not wish to offend so kind a master.

The old man looked at him shrewdly. "But you think it is a bad barter, all the same, do you not?" Master Crowe chuckled.

Duffy nodded sheepishly, and his teacher laughed again.

"Well, you're a truthful lad, and so it would be, a very bad barter, if this were indeed water as it seems to be. This, though, shall be your first lesson at my hands: *things are not always what they seem.* Watch this *water* of mine."

So saying, he took up a pair of tongs and lifted a rosy coal from the brazier and dipped it into the iron pot as if to quench it.

Instead of the hiss of steam that Duffy had expected, the water leapt up, kindled into blue flames!

Duffy drew in his breath sharply. As each new silver drop fell from the spout above, it, too, burst afire, until the walls danced with eerie shadows. In the darkness behind the weird flickering, a spill of ghastly blue light fell across one of the liquid-filled bottles Duffy had noticed the day before. A dusky-colored serpent hung suspended in it like a constellation in the chill night sky, and its cold and sleepless eyes seemed to look through the flames and into Duffy's brain.

In the midst of the spectacle of water-blue fire, Master Crowe spoke gently and put a comforting arm around Duffy's rigid shoulders. "Lose your fear, Duffy. This seems to you now to be a trick, some unnatural magic. My child, it is not so."

"How . . . do you do it, Master?" Duffy asked then.

"This is not a new secret of my own invention. Many have seen it. You are not the first to think it beyond the plan of heaven that water should burn like dry wood. But you have much to learn concerning how wonderful *and* how terrible is the world."

The last drops of the burning water had now been spent, and the blue flames flickered out. The dim charcoal fire seemed cozy by comparison, but a little dull.

"I will tell you something now, boy, and I think you are a stout enough fellow not to take fright of it." Master Crowe dismantled his equipment as he spoke, handing pieces to Duffy to be replaced on their proper shelves. "You are here to learn the arts of an apothecary. It is an admirable profession, for many are every day and everywhere ill or discomforted and in need of healing medicine.

"But I think you are a bright boy, and curious, and perhaps also brave and strong. I should like to teach you my other profession as well. I am myself more than an apothecary. I am an alchemist."

Now, *this* was easy enough for Duffy to believe. He had just witnessed his master's strange magic only minutes before. And though the other almshouse boys had seemed frightened of alchemy, believing it evil and dangerous, and alchemists summoners of ghosts and demons from hell, Duffy did not believe that. He thought of only one thing he knew about alchemists.

"Hurrah!" he cried. "Master, I will do all you say, for I would dearly love to change things into gold!"

For a moment, Master Crowe looked stern. But his face softened presently. "The child is young," he said as if to himself. "He will learn."

He put a hand on Duffy's shoulder and asked mildly, "Have you seen any gold, then, in my house?"

Truly, this was a puzzle. Duffy looked around.

"No, sir, no gold. Nor any finery." He did not add, *Nor the comforts one might expect to find in the lodgings of a great magician.* He did not have to. There was hardly as much luxury as one might expect of a busy apothecary.

"Remember, child, what I have taught you already. Things are not always what they seem. It is true I am an alchemist, and I have some knowledge, at least, of where to look for that great treasure, the Jewel of Life, the Philosophers' Stone. It is a great and miraculous thing, the Stone, and it promises power and wealth to the one who finds it where it nestles among the commonplace.

"Even to some alchemists it appears that making plain gold is the secret of power and wealth, and they search for herbs and amulets that will convert lead into coin. But would you put such a value on your life? After all, the king's donkey wears a halter of gold! The treasure we seek is not such ordinary stuff."

Duffy's heart wilted with disappointment, and his face showed it. Apparently, Master Crowe was not the sort of sorcerer who could have money at his fingertips. It was really too bad, for Duffy would have liked to be wealthy and important. He sighed.

Master Crowe lifted Duffy up onto the table, so that their faces were opposite one another, and Duffy was surprised at the strength in the old man's frail-seeming body.

"Come now," Master Crowe said. "Your face is overlong. Be of good cheer. Are not the stars and angels of heaven much prettier than anything a rich man might buy? Believe me when I tell you that alchemy is a most wonderful science, for it teaches a person to mine and smelt and to work the gold of his own heart and soul. *That* is a treasure that cannot be spent or stolen."

"I'm not quite sure I understand, sir. Is it a riddle?"

Master Crowe shook his head.

But there had been comfort in the old man's speech and kindness in his touch. Duffy had come to that much of a conclusion, at least. So he spoke one of his secrets aloud.

"I think I could stand better being poor, after all, if I am to be taught about stars and angels. I saw an angel in a glass window, once, with a crown of stars."

The angel had had wings of light-pierced blue-green feathers. She'd been holding a sandglass in her left hand, and a sword in her right, and light had streamed from her face and from the golden mountain on which she stood. The bright memory of the angel mixed in Duffy's mind with Master Crowe's words about wealth and power and the Philosophers' Stone. There was so much to learn, so much to understand!

"Master," he said after a moment's more thought, "teach me whatever art you will, for I would be an alchemist just like you."

CHAPTER 4

DEVIL'S OWN

UFFY FOUND, DURING THE REST OF THAT DAY, that even the ordinary tasks of life at Master Crowe's were not an apprentice's usual boring chores. Marketing became an adventure as the old man led the way, not to the open stalls in the center of town, but to shabby little shops hidden away in closed alleys. Here, scrawny dogs whined at Duffy's heels, and dark-browed strangers wheedled for better prices for the goods that Master Crowe bought from them: a lump of amber-colored resin, from a dark, small woman who wore a tattered shawl over her head and a golden ring through one side of her nose; a bundle of dried roots, from a tow-headed man whose words were thick with an outlander's accent; a half-polished piece of greenish stone speckled as if with drops of blood, from a woman who might have been any farmer's wife, except for the scar on her right cheek where she had been branded for thievery.

Around midday, Duffy noticed uneasily that Master Crowe was taking him to the only corner of Elford that the almshouse boys avoided.

"Are we going into Devil's Own?" Duffy asked, giving the

sorry place the name he'd heard in the almshouse, and remembering with fear that conversation.

"They'll only cut your purse—if luck is *with* you," George Tallow had said, grinning unpleasantly at the younger boys. "If you're out of luck, more likely it will be your throat."

Another boy had added, "The only ones who live there are the foreigners. We won't have their like in the middle of Elford Town."

Yet Duffy had great confidence in his master. Old though he might be, Crowe could cause water to burn. So he was a powerful magician, and an underling could always depend on such a master's protection.

Crowe seemed untroubled by the hooded glances that fell on them. And Duffy held his own head up, trying to look careless and at ease, though the tightness at the back of his neck reminded him that he was still very much afraid.

The old man stopped for a moment to buy horseradishes from a toothless root man. While Duffy stood waiting, he listened nervously to two men standing hard by. They were speaking in some heathen language, and one of them looked sharply at Duffy once or twice, clearly judging whether or not he understood any of it. Duffy's expression must have satisfied the man, though, for he turned his back and went on speaking.

The two men went from quiet conversation into sudden disagreement, the peculiar language rising to sharp, throaty barks. Abruptly, one man yanked off his hat in anger, and something that had been in it flew out and fell silently in the dust at Duffy's feet. It lay for only a second, a hoop of bright yellow metal, before Duffy set his foot over it. Heart pounding, he gazed upward as if nothing had happened.

But he *had* been seen. His eyes met another pair of eyes, and terror seized him.

On the ledge of the closest house, above the heads of the arguing foreigners, was a devil. It was only about as big as a baby, but covered with scurfy brown hair, and not wearing any clothes. It had the face of an old man. Duffy did not notice devilish horns on its forehead, but he could see it had a long tail and sharp, yellow teeth, which showed when it leered at him.

Duffy knew immediately that the imp had seen him step on the ring, and he shuddered, regretting his sly act. "*Wicked deeds, Wickedness breeds,*" he murmured. It was a pious catchphrase of Master Humphrey's, usually preached during a beating.

When the devil reached down to an open shutter beneath the ledge and swung itself close to where he stood, Duffy leapt back. The ring was almost buried in the dust, ground in by his foot, but the devil saw it and, hanging down by one long arm, hooked it up with a black-nailed finger. The creature laughed—at least, Duffy supposed that short, hissing noise was a laugh—and swung back up to its ledge. Biting the ring once, the imp then withdrew into a shadowed niche in the wall.

No one in the alley except Duffy seemed to have seen it, but now the foreign man with the cap was shouting. He yelled and shook his fist, shoving the cap in the other man's face. This other waved his arms wildly, turned his own pockets inside out, said something emphatic, and pointed to Master Crowe. Now that Duffy had moved aside to avoid the devil, the old man was the person standing closest to them.

In a few strides, the two men closed in on Crowe, and though they spoke with heavy accents, Duffy understood what they were saying only too well.

"Give it back, old man, if you don't want trouble. Your grey beard won't protect you here. Give it back, quick now!"

"I have nothing of yours," Master Crowe said.

"None of that!"

Duffy thought they were going to strike his master, and he saw that Crowe seemed helpless before their rage. Could the old man not cast some spell on them? Duffy waited a heartbeat more before giving up on that hope, then cried out desperately, "He hasn't got it!"

"What's that?"

"*What* hasn't he got, brat?"

Now Duffy found himself the center of attention, and he heartily wished he could have kept his mouth shut.

"You've got it, then? Hand it over!"

"No, I . . . haven't." Duffy thought guiltily that he almost *had* been the thief. But that was not what mattered. What was he going to say to these angry men? He couldn't think fast enough.

"Hand it over!" The man in the cap grabbed Duffy's shoulder and gave it a rough shake.

"I haven't got your ring," Duffy cried. "The . . . the devil took it up there!" He pointed to the ledge, but there was no longer any figure leering down at him.

"Hold your lies!" But the man saw that Duffy's eyes stayed fixed on the place he had pointed out. "Is the lad simple?" he demanded of Crowe. "Or is this some trick?"

"Look there," Crowe said sharply. "He's not simple."

The men looked back at the ledge again, and this time they all saw what Duffy had seen before: a wizened manikin grinning and clutching a gold ring.

The men did not stay to talk. They fled outright.

To Duffy's astonishment, Crowe began to chuckle. "A devil. He looks like a devil, yes, boy, he certainly does. But he's only an ape. Come along, Duffy. As it happens, we have business with him already."

Reluctantly, Duffy followed Crowe to a flight of stairs that went up the side of the very building the creature seemed to haunt. The thing had disappeared again before they got to the age-blackened door at the top of the steps.

Before the apothecary had a chance to rap, the door was opened.

"Welcome, Master Crowe," came a soft, high voice, and they went in.

Chapter 5

Master Wing

T WAS A SHADOWY ROOM, NOT REALLY A shop at all. There were frayed tapestries on the walls, and a carpet, faded and soft, on the uneven floor.

The man who had opened the door and spoken in such a reedy voice did not look like anyone Duffy had ever seen in Elford. His skin was taut and golden, his black eyes set between slanted lids. In the usual scholarly fashion, his coat was cut long and full, but it was of a lustrous, dark violet-blue, brocaded with tarnished silver in a pattern of swallows and flowering branches. The man's feet were shod in felt slippers which curled up at the toe.

It was clear that he had been expecting their visit, for wordlessly he indicated a table where three illuminated manuscripts were laid out in a row, ready for inspection.

Master Crowe, as silent as his host, seated himself in a heavy armchair and began to examine them. He did not say anything more about the creature on the ledge. He did not discuss the queer pictures that decorated the pages he held. And for once, he failed to make even a passing remark to reassure his apprentice. He was so absorbed in what he was doing that he seemed to forget Duffy.

Duffy wanted to trust his master, but he was terribly afraid of the demon. Crowe had called it an ape. Duffy knew there were beasts called apes, though he had never seen one, but surely no harmless animal could look so maliciously human.

The air of the apartment was thick with some sort of sweet, drowsy incense, and Duffy felt that the impassive yellow man who lived there was watching him—not with malevolence, perhaps, and maybe not even with interest, but watching him nonetheless. When the mysterious foreigner glided out of the room, Duffy sighed out loud, feeling both relieved and newly apprehensive.

When the man returned, the hairy figure with him was unmistakable. In fact, it was still carrying the ring. Now, though, it was wearing a collar and a leash.

Duffy dared a look at the ape. Even more bravely, he stepped nearer to it. That close, the ape seemed to lose some of its gargoyle fiendishness. Duffy's devil, clearly, was the yellow man's pet.

When his host set the ape on the floor, it arched its back and took a few stiff-legged, menacing steps toward Duffy, growling and stretching its lips so its sharp teeth glittered. Duffy stumbled backward, but the man was making soothing gestures toward him with one hand and tugging gently at the leash with the other.

Looking over its shoulder at its master, the ape twittered some kind of comment. Then abruptly it sat down, with its knees folded up against its chest, its eyebrows working up and down. Elaborately ignoring Duffy, it held the gold ring up and examined it, passing it from one hand to the other, sniffing at it, tapping the ring on its knee, puckering up its lips, and delicately licking the golden hoop. But it did not think much of how the ring tasted, for it made a face and threw the thing down. When the ring rolled a few inches, the ape snatched it up again in leathery, black fingers, clutching it to its cheek. Then, dropping its pretense of ignoring Duffy, it looked right at him, fluttering its eyelids like a moonstruck milkmaid and making a soft, chirping noise with its pouching lips.

Duffy smiled tentatively. *After all,* he asked himself, *how could such a silly creature be frightening?* At his smile, the ape gracefully curled its tail around the leash. Then it unfolded one long leg and scratched industriously at some vermin behind its ear, before turning away from Duffy and languorously stretching its back.

The yellow man held the leash handle out to Duffy then and made a scratching motion with his other hand toward the ape's back. "He desires you to help him reach the places he cannot see. He desires your friendship." The yellow man's way of saying words made them all sound as if they curled at the end the way his carpet slippers did.

"*My* friendship?"

The yellow man nodded.

Duffy touched the long fur timidly at first. But then he realized from the way the ape comfortably rolled its thin, muscular trunk, that a good scratching was just what it wanted. He worked his fingernails up and down the ape's back and grinned. By and by, Duffy was even feeding the ape from a plate of grapes provided for him.

Master Crowe finally looked up from his study and motioned to his apprentice to come over and look at the cockled sheets of vellum.

"Visiting Master Wing is always a mixed pleasure," Crowe said with a rueful smile. "He deals only in the finest works, and my purse is always too light to do the service I would like. All three of these paintings could teach us much, Duffy, if we had the time to study them carefully."

Duffy looked at the figures on the parchment closest to him. They had been sketched in brown ink and shaded with dark red chalk: a man in a winged hat, an egg with a rayed sun for its yolk, and a light brown crown inside which curled a snake, its tail in its own mouth. Duffy could make nothing of any of it. He wondered if he was expected to comment on what he was shown, and he felt rather ignorant. The images seemed to have nothing to do with one another. They were like fragments of a dream.

Without explaining the first picture, Master Crowe held out the second.

This one was simpler, Duffy thought, but no less bizarre. It showed a large glass bottle, stoppered at the top. Inside the bottle, two dogs, a black one and a white, were engaged in a terrible battle. Blood from their innumerable bites and scratches pooled in the bottom of the jar. It was a painful puzzle . . . and yet . . . Duffy frowned thoughtfully. He almost had a feeling that he might have some idea of what sort of story would go with this picture.

Master Crowe smiled at Duffy's consternation. "Your face, child, has the ability to grow long on very short notice. What if I were to tell you that there are secret messages hidden in these pictures, and that learning to read them will be a large part of your work with me?"

Secret messages, magical animals, brown crowns. *Secret messages!* Duffy caught his breath. He did not think these were things which most people in Elford discussed readily. He was sure Master Humphrey, the almshouse beadle, did not have much to say about matters of this sort! *To think,* he said to himself, *I might have been only Mistress Cotter's page, and never have heard of these wonders. . . .*

"I believe," he said slowly to Master Crowe, "it will take me a long time to understand it all."

Master Crowe did not reply as if he were speaking to an underling, but with a level answer. "It may well be part of the magic that we *never* understand it all. But we will make a start."

He laid the third page before his apprentice. "We will at any rate begin with a message more basic than these first two. Look here."

Duffy had thought the morning's experiment a marvel, had sensed a knotted magic in the symbols of the other manuscripts. But those paled beside this third illumination. Something of this beauty went past his puzzling thoughts and straight into his heart.

The picture was of a dancer, poised on one foot, with arms flung up and out, as if mid-swirl. In his left hand was a curved sword; the right held a rose, white where its petals unfolded, crimson at its still budlike heart. The dancer's hair was dark, lit golden by a burst of radiance. The eyes of the dancer were open wide, as if they could take in the whole glory of the world, and of other worlds as well. All around spun sun and moon and showers of stars, red and green and white, and beams from them touched the dancer's hands and feet, brow and breast and belly, as if the whole dance were held up and bathed in light.

The joy Duffy felt was such a simple joy, as if the sun had come out from behind a mist—but nothing in his life up to that point had been so totally untroubled. Where, in the ordinary pattern of days and work and nights and rest could this bliss be found again, this sense of harmony?

He gazed at the dancing figure for a long time. Finally, words found him, and scarcely knowing that he spoke, he said, "The magic—it's all like that, then?"

It was Master Wing who answered first, his voice soft and grave. "Magic? All *Life* is like that, at the heart. As it is above, so it is below."

The ape, who had been on the carpet, reached out a long arm and pulled itself onto the table, then scrambled onto Wing's shoulder. Wing seemed accustomed to the move, and he went on as though it were nothing unusual. "Mortals say the stars act for good or ill, or that they do so themselves; it is all the same. In heaven and on earth, in dream and in daylight, the song of the stars may be heard. We are our own stars. The dance and the dancer are the same."

Master Crowe nodded. "This is the only absolute law of alchemy, my boy: All things grow toward perfection. The ore in the earth, the child in Elford, the angel in heaven—to hear them growing is to hear the Great Music.

"And know this, too," he added. "This is also the practical rule for herbs and healing: Curse and cure align in harmony with the planets. It is helpful to know that herbs of Mars, for instance, are those that strengthen or heal those parts of the body which are also of Mars—as honeysuckle balm, for one, will cure a headache. But in our most true experiments we may someday do much more. For, in finding the Philosophers' Stone, we will also find the Panacea, the medicine that cures *all* ills—and the Elixir of Life Eternal. The three are found together."

Master Crowe paused then, for he saw that Duffy was not conscious of his words. The dancer on the page had all his attention, and his face was rapt and happy.

Master Wing and the apothecary Crowe looked at one another.

"We may hear Truth anywhere," said Master Wing. "Fortunate are those who recognize that Voice. You are blessed in your apprentice."

Duffy, though, just looked at the picture of the graceful figure with the sword and the rose, and smiled.

CHAPTER 6

THE DUSTY BOTTLE

BACK AT THE APOTHECARY SHOP ONCE MORE, they found three customers waiting, two to buy and one to beg remedies. Master Jarrett's quinsy was worse, his daughter said. And Madge Miller wanted catnip tea for her scullery maid's headache. An old woman with an earache offered to sweep the steps for a bit of sweet oil, but Crowe told her to take it home directly and rest until it had done its work. By this time, more folk had come by, and the afternoon business was brisk.

"Until we discover the Panacea," Master Crowe promised, "I will keep you busy, young Duffy."

Duffy ran here and there fetching things, and climbed up and down the ladder so many times to reach jars on the top shelf that he began to wonder what cure Crowe had for sore legs. He wished that he himself were an ape, with long, sure fingers and toes and a tail that would make light work of swinging across the shop and balancing near the ceiling.

When at last Master Crowe saw that Duffy was tired, he showed him how to measure herbs in the balance scales. The metal weights went on one side: the grain-sized ones molded like barleycorns, the scruples like almonds, the drams, walnuts, and the ounces like little cats. When the proper amount of herbs had been scooped into the pan on the other side, the weighted pan came teeter-tottering up, and the two pans hung exactly even on either side of the scale's standard.

"And now we grind the coarse leaves, twigs, bark, and roots in the mortar," Crowe said during a lull between customers. He showed Duffy both mortar and pestle and the quick little turns of the wrist that made powder of the herbs. Next he demonstrated how to tie the powdered herbs into small linen bags.

Duffy gratefully sat down to this soothing task. Some of the herbs were strong and pungent; a few smelled awful. He couldn't understand how the foul, stinking drugs could help people feel better, unless the herbs were to be burned for smoke to chase a pestilence away. But one or two of the herbs were fresh as a mown meadow, sweet and minty, delightful to handle. Whenever Duffy came across one of these he would lean over and breathe in the clean aroma, these sweet airs refreshing him.

"So," he said to himself proudly, "already I know half of this trade. Now I have only to learn the use of bitter herbs, and I, too, will be able to call myself apothecary."

At sundown, Master Crowe pulled closed the heavy shutters of the shop windows.

"I think you have brought me luck, Duffy," he said. "Scarcely can I recall a better afternoon's business in all the years I have kept shop here in Elford Town. Nor did any come for grave illness, but most for strewing herbs and stewing spices and such—more luck. Truly, if this continues, the other herbalists will be wondering what secrets of healing old Crowe is dispensing, that everyone flocks to him so." The moment's mood was merry. "I think we should celebrate and show heaven we notice well how we have been blessed." He paused and looked thoughtful.

Duffy was learning to recognize this habit of his master's, of gazing past the company and objects at hand and into hollow air, as if some notion were becoming visible to him there.

"Let us find a lesson in this, my boy. The wise ones say, 'The three birds hatch and fly together.' The Red Bird, now, is your Soul, and the White Bird is your Spirit. 'But the Black Bird is the Body, which dwelleth on the Earth, yet that Bird also shall most assuredly fly. . . .' *What* can that mean, really? These sayings are not foolishness, of that I am sure. Well, I can see this talk of birds is beyond you this evening."

Duffy had, in fact, yawned.

"I mean to say, I think we should have a fine dinner tonight and coddle ourselves a bit. What would you say to a gooseberry pie from Mistress Wheat's cookshop? Is that the kind of bird talk you can understand?"

Duffy had never tasted gooseberry pie, and his mouth fairly watered at the thought of the flaky crusts he had seen in the shop window, the glistening sweetness bubbling out through the designs pierced in the pastry, while the escaping steam curled about like clouds at high summer. To eat such a dinner seemed likely to be as much of an adventure as anything that had happened to him since he had come to be apprenticed.

Crowe saw the spark of eagerness in Duffy's eyes and laughed. "That suits you, eh? Well, I shall fetch it home as soon as can be, hot from the goodwife's oven. Do you, Duffy, while I am gone, hasten downstairs and tidy a place for our banquet. We can't have dust falling on so royal a meal, now can we?"

"Indeed no, sir," Duffy answered, trying to sound as adult as he felt a successful merchant ought.

Master Crowe went out, and Duffy clattered down the old stairs, humming a bit of a tune he had heard a shepherd singing in the market square.

He went first to peek at the tin box in the rubbish. The stoat was coiled, asleep. Duffy thought he might at least pet her, but he was too hasty. His wrist brushed against the box, and Iseult was jarred awake. She hissed at him.

As he hadn't any food at hand, Duffy merely looked at her for a moment more. Then he went to his work, promising as he tucked her away, "I'll save you a bit of pie. George wouldn't have done that, would he?"

The table was covered with delicate blown-glass beakers, pottery bowls, and bottles, as well as the boxes of herbs that Crowe had been blending all afternoon. Duffy moved carefully and quickly, pleased to think how well he was working.

"I wonder," he said aloud, "how an old man like Master Crowe managed to run the shop before he had someone to help him." It didn't occur to Duffy that when Master Crowe had left for Mistress Wheat's, he had actually looked less fatigued than his apprentice. "Hugh and Bertie and the others at the almshouse will be impressed when I tell them how important it is to be an apothecary," Duffy said, as much to Iseult as to himself. "Even George Tallow might give me a little respect."

And of course, he thought, *there is the magic. But I shan't tell them about that. At least, not yet!*

He found a scrap of rag and dusted the table, and then in a fit of thoroughness, he fetched out the water bucket from the cubby in the floor and washed the tabletop until not a speck of dirt clung to it.

Still Master Crowe had not returned, and Duffy looked about for something more to occupy him while he waited, something to keep his mind off the rumbling of his stomach and the delicious, melting flavor of gooseberry pie that he could almost taste.

His eyes roamed about the dank corners of the cellar, and then fell slowly, as if drawn by a lodestone, on the dusty bottle that held the snake.

"That bottle is dirty," Duffy said to himself. "I ought to clean it. I'll be able to see the snake better if I do."

Slowly, he walked around the table, the damp rag still in his hand. He knew the snake was only a dead thing—killed by a cat, Master Crowe had told him, and preserved in liquor. But Duffy felt a shiver run up his spine and out into his shoulders, just as if the snake had been watching him.

"It's only because the eyes aren't closed," he whispered to reassure himself. "There's nothing really strange about it."

He stood before the shelf and wiped the jar with his rag. The dust had lain thick on the rounded surface, and now he could see much more clearly the enameled patterns of brown and grey, black and cream, winding across the serpent's backbone and cupping down tight to a scaled, lipless smile that barely showed the slender fangs.

The lidless eyes stared, and Duffy felt for a second the horror of floating forever, steeped through to the bone in a stagnant ocean no larger than a glass bottle.

But the snake is dead, he thought. *It can't see me out here, it can't see outside the jar.*

The snake seemed to rise and fall gently on some mysterious tide, and Duffy rubbed his eyes. The water in the bottle could not be moving, and the snake was not alive. Yet surely there was a tide, for Duffy felt it washing over him, slow and soft as a sleeping breath.

"But I am outside," Duffy murmured dimly.

The serpent eyes stared, and Duffy wondered at how strange he felt, pressed down gently by fathoms of insistent, flowing water. It was so much trouble to stand upright, to keep his feet under him. He reached for something to hold onto, his arm moving slowly, graceful and aimless as flooded sedge. When he turned to look around, pushing his face and shoulders against the flow, he still half expected to see the dusty corners of the cellar somewhere behind him. But there were no corners, for the ocean was boundless.

CHAPTER 7

THE SERPENT OUTSIDE OF TIME

BEHIND HIM, DUFFY FELT THE EYES OF THE snake: still passive, still floating, still watching and possessing his every movement. Somewhere behind his ribs, Duffy knew, there was a swelling kernel of panic that would burst any moment. If that moment would only come, the fear would break loose and he would find a way to escape those staring eyes.

But right now he couldn't run. The fear wouldn't blossom and defend him.

Under his feet, the infinite silver sands danced like slow galaxies, and Duffy watched the rippling patterns until he knew every star, every cloudy nebula, every planet and moon spelled out by the silently shifting dunes.

How far behind him were those watching eyes? Duffy didn't know. There was no distance here in the endless sea. Duffy felt his panic stir like live seed under the earth. He turned to look. There was the mirthless smile of the serpent, there were the rune-like markings of dark and light scales layered on one another. There were the eyes. With a shock, Duffy thought of the filminess clearing from them; he thought of them glinting like splinters of smoky crystal.

Terror began to push into his throat. Now, finally, time and will flowed back into him. He knew he must escape.

He began to run. He *wanted* to run, to feel his legs pumping as fast as his heart was beating. But the water was pulling at him like invisible hands, holding him back. The sand shifted under him and would give him no firm footing. It seemed as if the whole ocean were fighting him, dragging him back toward that silent horror. There was no escape.

The amber water thickened about Duffy once more, and the seconds were beginning to spin out into eternities. His feet no longer yearned to run, his breathing no longer came in gasps. Behind him, the snake floated, its lipless mouth curved into a smile.

What would it be like, Duffy wondered, watching the sand ripple gently, *What would it be like not to struggle?* He almost began to relax into his death.

Master Crowe's voice sounded then, thin and hopelessly far away. Or perhaps Duffy was only dreaming that someone was calling his name.

Still, he thought, *if it is only a dream, a loud noise will wake me.*

It was all so dim and confusing. He wished the voice were louder, and, yes, there it was again, stronger this time, filtering through his brain like a net sinking through fathoms of stagnant water.

"Duffy! Where are you, child? Answer me!"

Was the voice coming from above? Was it not a dream after all? Duffy turned to look around him, and the golden sea cleared. The snake, though still there, was far away and small with the distance. And now Duffy could see, too, between the snake and himself, something that did not waver like the ocean currents: a solid curve of glass. The snake hung suspended in a glass jar, and Duffy was on the outside once more.

The voice was clearer now, and there were other sounds: Master Crowe's boots thudding rapidly down the stairs from the shop, and a hesitant tapping at the back of the cellar where a barred wicket opened on the alley.

Master Crowe's cloak was half off from his dash down the stair, and his white hair stood on end like so much cottonweed down.

"Duffy!" he cried, "Are you all right? You gave me a turn by not answering, child. But hurry, now, to the back gate, and let in the poor fellow who's knocking, before someone sees him."

Nothing could have suited Duffy better. He wanted fresh air above all things. The tapping had stopped by this time, and he ran down the cellar's length and flung open the gate.

At first he saw no one as he stood gulping in air that suddenly seemed sweet as clover, for all that there was an open ditch running through the uncobbled alleyway. Presently, though, a bit of shadow crept forward from the wall opposite and, with a sudden snatch at quickness, darted past him into the safe gloom of the hallway behind.

Chapter 8

Djano the Vagabond

THE MAN'S CLOTHES WERE DIRTY, ALMOST grey, but Duffy could see that they had once been gay with color. Even here, in the heavy air of the cellar, the tatters and tags seemed about to flutter. A bit of bedraggled ribbon, that might have called itself scarlet, swayed ever so slightly. The fellow was lean and feline, with sun-browned skin and uncombed black hair. In his arms, he cradled a fretful baby whose eyes peered out like Iseult's, from within her blanket.

It was clear from the man's motley costume that he was a traveling player, and Duffy now understood the secrecy of this visit. For some years, the magistrates had outlawed players from coming into Elford. They charged that the players' frivolous tunes and puppet shows caused people to leave off business and necessary work, as if any day the players chose to appear became a festival day. The magistrates maintained that the children would be pestering their parents and the dogs barking continuously. Furthermore, the horses bred by some of the wanderers and sold to settled folk never seemed to stay safely stabled, but at the first chance ran back to the players.

It was three summers since Duffy had heard any merry pipes and fiddles in the market square.

Composing himself after his nervous dash, the man murmured to his infant, "Ah, Nania, hush, hush." Then he reached into the bosom of his ragged shirt. With the grace of a conjuror, he drew out a little green parrot with a plum-colored head and a long, turquoise tail, which settled itself on his thumb.

"There now," he said to the bird. "No hiding your pretty coat here. We are with friends." His voice rolled and glimmered with a marked accent.

By this time, Duffy was feeling much better, and he longed to touch those gleaming feathers, and to feel the parrot's little claws curled around his own finger. He remembered his manners, though, and his duties as Master Crowe's servant.

"Come this way, please," he said in an official tone, and led the way down the cellar toward the workroom.

The tattered stranger followed several diffident paces behind, still crooning to the baby and to the bird.

Crowe was whisking here and there, pulling down jars and measuring dabs and pinches of the different herbs into the mortar to be ground and mixed. He looked up at their entrance and nodded.

Clearly, Duffy thought, *he recognizes the man.*

The player bobbed his head once. "My Nania coughs," he said. "My friend Wing, he tells me you will help."

"Master Djano, you say the baby coughs?" Crowe asked, gently teasing the infant's mouth open to look inside.

"Master, she coughs so she cannot sleep, poor child. I am at my wit's end."

"And is the cough dry and hoarse, or wet and choking?"

"Dry, Master, and you see her poor throat is red and raw. Since my woman died I have tried to be both mother and father to the babe, but I have no knowledge of these things. I do my tricks for her, I pull silk handkerchiefs from the air. I crack eggs and show her buttercups inside where the meat should be. I make her smile, but then she coughs and coughs again, and if she cannot laugh, it must be that her throat hurts. I would rather see the sun swallowed in the sky than see her hurt so. Please, Master, you must make my baby well. She is my treasure, she is all I have in the world."

Crowe crumbled dried sprigs into the mortar as he listened. A piney scent came from the leaves, and he muttered under his breath, "Ahh, just so. You must put yourself at ease," he added, to Djano. "She has not the signs of the fever nor of the plague. She'll mend soon. Now, Duffy, this is rosemary, you see, good for sore throat. These . . ." he pointed to some withered, purplish nuggets ". . . these are rose fruit, also a surpassing anodyne. Powder them fine." As he spoke, he ground the herbs himself. "And this is coltsfoot—*'Foul oil of Rue for the sinew's cramp. Coltsfoot for coughing and chill of damp.'* " His dry old voice half sang, half recited the words.

"We have our music, too," he remarked, smiling, to the player. "Not so sweet as yours, I know, but worthy. Duffy, I'll teach you this bit. Or some of it. The next line goes—let me see—*'Centaury cools fever. Poppy brings sleep. Foxglove the failing heart will keep.'* Ah, remind me to tell you about foxglove, Duffy. There, now," he added, dumping the last of the mixture into a cloth sack and tying it securely. "This will do very well, I think. Brew it into a strong tea and give it to her to drink for three days. You might also try to find some wild honey to mix with it—it's somewhat bitter for a young one. And give her oatmeal instead of milk for nourishment, if you can. But if it must be milk, try to get some from a young sheep, not from a cow. Do this and you will cure her cough, I promise you."

Djano took the packet of herbs he was offered, but for a minute he did not speak. The baby coughed, and poked one tiny fist out of the blanket, waving it at her father's face. He looked down at her, and then at the apothecary.

"Master," he said finally, "you are the only one in this town besides Master Wing who has been kind to a stranger. I thank you indeed. But still, that is nothing, I am long used to abuse and suspicion here in Elford. It is a player's normal lot in this land. Kindness to my child, though . . ." He shook his head sadly. "Elford mothers with babes of their own have turned us from their doors, thinking my Nania coughed with the plague. Fathers have set dogs at my heels when I begged bread for my sick child. Yes, I *begged*—I, Djano, son of Alonzo!" For a moment there was a defiant fire in his eyes, and embattled pride in his voice. "My father performed for the King of Spain! And I with him!" he squared his shoulders, and the pride faded into anger. "Now I beg here in Elford. I would rather see the sun swallowed in the sky than beg, I had thought. But when I must—what else is there to do? The townspeople will not let me put on my show. Season by season, I arrive in other towns and find they have followed Elford's hardhearted magistrates. They treat me as an outlaw. They will not give me even pennies for the rhymes and songs a player is born to. Did my father have a garden to leave me, did he have a barn for me to fill?" His words rushed on, his accent and his emotion tangling them and tripping him up. "They drive me from the town and force me to hide as you have yourself seen. And now, when you alone have done something to ease my child's misery, I haven't a coin to give you. I cannot pay for this medicine."

Crowe shook his head gently at the poor man's distress. "You have enough to worry about, surely, without concerning yourself with payment. Have I said anything about money? Your friend Wing is my friend also, and he did well to send you to me. Besides, these herbs are all so common I have but to gather them by the roadside. They cost me nothing. If Nature is kind enough to give them to me, why, surely I can give them to you as well. Believe me, if folk but troubled to know the virtue in simple weeds and grasses, there'd be so few coughing babes and unsettled stomachs, I could spend my time napping in the sun."

The bird on Djano's sleeve stretched her wings just then, ruffling and then refolding them neatly. She sidled over by his ear and, to Duffy's great astonishment, spoke.

"King of Spain," she said, *"Rey d'España. Buttercups in the sun."*

As the player regarded the little parrot, the shame in Djano's face gave way to pride once more, and even to gaiety.

"Hold!" he urged suddenly. "I *do* have something I can give." With tenderness, he lifted the parrot on one finger, like a living bijou, and caressed her silken feathers. "I have had Pajara for three years, Master. I bought her in Spain with a golden coin given me by the King's daughter. She gave it me when I performed at court on the feast day of Saint James." He sighed. "I have come down in the world since then. But Pajara!" He smiled. "She can do turns to amuse the very sky. She speaks words she has heard only two, maybe three, times. She can speak in four tongues. My woman taught her that."

As Djano spoke, he deftly settled the baby Nania, still wrapped in her blanket, against the foot of Duffy's pallet and flung off his own cloak. "No one in this unfortunate town has heard players' music for years, now, but you shall not be so luckless. I will play and sing for you and your lad, good Master, and Pajara will dance. And when I go, you will have her, Master, with my thanks. Look, she is as beautiful as the moon."

Crowe did not speak immediately, and Djano added anxiously, "She need not be a care to you. She is worth a lot of money, sire. Perhaps you could sell her to some kind and wealthy woman. It would surely pay for the medicine."

Master Crowe held out a wrinkled hand, and the parrot stepped daintily onto it.

"Sell her?" said Master Crowe in soft denial. "I would not sell a bird as beautiful as the moon."

CHAPTER 9

WORRIES AND WARNINGS

UFFY LAY AWAKE LATE THAT NIGHT, THOUGH he was so tired his head ached and the delicate gooseberry pie lumped in his stomach like so much wet wool. He had thought Master Crowe surely noticed something amiss when he returned home from the cookshop and found his apprentice dazed and mute. But in the business of preparing medicine for the player's baby, and the delight of Djano's music and juggling and sleight of hand, the apothecary seemed to have forgotten his concern.

Once the ragged visitors were gone, Master Crowe's talk through dinner and the rest of the evening had all been of herbs and experiments to be tried, stories about the faraway places the spices came from, and lessons to be demonstrated. He'd had Duffy repeat and repeat the healing rhymes about coltsfoot and foxglove and others as well.

" '*Of burns, bugs, and skin sores,*' " Duffy obediently sang, " '*the sovereigns are: Aloes, and Houseleeks, and Juniper Tar.*' "

Crowe nodded as soon as Duffy had gotten all the words right twice. Then it was, "Oh, and here's one that is exceedingly useful: '*Salep of Orchis feeds delicate bellies. Bound ones take blackberry roots, teas, or jellies.*' Hmm? Try saying that once or twice."

He had appeared to give Duffy a sharp look every now and again, but Duffy supposed he could be imagining that. Still, he felt bewildered and distracted, and only half heard the queer fables Master Crowe told about black Ethiopes and royal marriages, terrible serpent kings, cockatrices, and dragons. One story caught his ear briefly because it reminded him of the manuscript he had seen in Devil's Own: it was something to do with a dragon that swallowed its own tail. But thinking about the dragon reminded Duffy too closely of the serpent's staring eyes in the bottle, and that only made him feel worse.

Now, huddled on his pallet in the dark, Duffy wondered if he should have told Master Crowe about what had occurred. Nothing of the sort had ever happened to him before, excepting nightmares. In daytime, awake, he had never been overtaken by such things. Duffy was fairly sure, tired though he had been, that he had not fallen asleep, for he had still been standing when Master Crowe came in.

In the hush and shadow of the cellar, fear now sat on Duffy's middle like a bully in an alley fight. He felt sick.

"Might Master Crowe have soothing words to cure fright and confusion?" he asked himself half aloud. "Or an herb salve for bruises of the mind?"

Yet surely, to tell such things as he had seen in the bottle would be a mistake. What could Master Crowe think of such an outlandish story? Duffy's miserable experience of life before yesterday didn't reassure him.

"He will think me a liar," he counseled himself. People always did expect almshouse boys to lie. "Or the Master might think it *was* all a nightmare, and that would not be good either." Only a lazy apprentice would have been sleeping when he was supposed to be tidying up. And perhaps he should not have meddled with the mysterious bottle at all. He hadn't been told to clean the shelf, only the table. Perhaps he should have realized that the cellar was full of magic and kept himself out of trouble.

"Better, far better, to tell nothing at all and say my prayers at night and keep my distance from that snake," he whispered, as if by saying the words out loud, it would all be true. Duffy shifted uncomfortably on his straw mattress, and the pie in his belly groaned and sighed.

" '*Salep of Orchis feeds delicate bellies,*' " he mumbled to himself. But he was too tired to try any remedy save that of holding still in the darkness.

His dreams that night, when he finally slept, were vivid and troublesome. He stood among the towering shelves, crowded on all sides by dark rainbows of bottles, forests of drying herbs. A procession of almond-eyed merchants wound toward him, carrying smoking pies that smelled of honey and incense.

"Now I shall eat," Duffy heard his own voice saying, but as the words left his mouth, the tallest merchant unaccountably turned into an Ethiope who fastened a black leash around Duffy's neck and chanted, "*Solve et coagula. Aurea progenies plumbo prognata parente.*"

The foreign sounds were disquieting, mysterious yet familiar. In his dream Duffy thought, *I must ask Master Crowe;* but when he tried to run to find the old man, the leash held him back, and he realized he would never be able to remember the words to ask about them. He turned to look at the Ethiope, but that person was nowhere to be seen. Instead, a small black bird held the end of the leash in one claw and said in the Ethiope's voice, "*En to pan. En to pan.* Djano, a song for the ladies! *Dia bellissima!*"

Duffy woke with a start to find Master Crowe in the room and the player's parrot hopping about, tweaking the blanket with her beak. She seemed delighted to see him open his eyes.

"Oh the sun, the sun," she chirped. "*Dia bellissima!*"

" '*Dia bellissima*' indeed!" Master Crowe laughed. "It is in truth a most lovely day, and I have just put the remains of last night's feast into the pan to warm. You have just time for a quick run down to the river and a spot of bathing before we break our fast. Indeed, it is a most lovely day."

The old man went upstairs then, and Duffy scrambled over to the rubbish corner. He had given Iseult a scrap of pie the night before and hidden another morsel under a heap of wilted sorrel leaves.

"Oh, you ate your dinner," he whispered, pleased to find not so much as a crumb left. The stoat stared at him and hissed. "I hope you are not starving. There's more, too," he went on hastily. "The way George took care of you, you must be used to being hungry. Look, here's some nice pie." But Iseult would not eat while he watched.

Duffy left the shop by the back gate and ran along the ditch toward the river. The sun was warm on his hair, and the dew already dry on the goose grass and fumiter that grew among the cobblestones.

Near the river, a housewife leaned out of an upper window and emptied a bucket of greasy water almost on Duffy's head, and he looked up to shout something rude at her. The words melted back onto his tongue, however, for as he looked up, he caught a glimpse of a stork winging overhead. It was headed for a messy pile of sticks against the chimney of Master Crowe's own rooftree. What luck! A stork's nest was the best sign going, everyone knew that. *Surely,* Duffy thought, *I was meant to be an apothecary, and an alchemist, too.* Soon he'd be having dainty berry pies every night, and maybe pudding as well.

At the water's edge, he pulled off his thick clothing and waded out where the river showed green and glassy and was deep enough for paddling and diving. A red and blue pleasure barge, decked with fluttering banners, drifted lazily downstream.

Shaking water from his ears, Duffy thought, *Were I to have a barge, it'd be grander than that old thing! T'would be yellow as tansy, and have gold railings, and I'd never go anywhere without musicians to play lutes and sing to me. And I'd have—*

Suddenly he felt something grip his ankle, and sky and river, barge and banks tipped madly and disappeared as green water closed over his head. He kicked and felt his free foot bump harmlessly against someone's leg. Then, choking and spluttering, his head was out of the water again.

George Tallow's shapeless mouth was smiling down at him unpleasantly.

"How's that for ducking, Master Wizard's Toad? I reckon you must be a slow learner, eh? Leastways, you don't float like a witch yourself—yet."

A shout of laughter went up from the muddy bank, and Duffy saw a straggling handful of other boys gathered there, watching. A couple were almshouse boys—Hugh and Bertie—but Duffy didn't know the rest. Bertie was looking at his feet, but Hugh actually spit on the ground.

"You look here when I'm talking, you little thief. Did you think I wouldn't know you were the one as took my stoat?" cried George. "You'd just better bring her back tonight, you little toad, or it won't go so well for you. Think you're so smart now you're an apprentice." George suddenly pushed Duffy's face into the water again and pulled him out by the hair. "Let this be a lesson to you. And you just try to learn the Evil Eye from your old man and see what it gets you. We won't stand for any of that in Elford, will we, boys?"

The boys cleared their throats and shook their heads. Hugh stuck out his chin and said, "We'll show him, won't we, George!"

"I reckon we will!" George called to them. "Just remember," he added to Duffy, staring him straight in the eye, "we'll have no old wizard calling his devils in Elford. And I'm not the only one as says so!"

CHAPTER 10

THE HUNGRY DEMON

LATER, BACK AT THE APOTHECARY'S CELLAR, Duffy recounted the episode carefully. George didn't *really* care about the stoat, he told himself, so he needn't mention her to Crowe. But the boys had thrown all his clothes into the water, and Duffy had to explain that much, at least. Besides, the names they had called him gnawed at his feelings.

"George heard that old busybody Cotter talking, I think," he told Crowe, managing to make his uncertainty sound like indignation. "As if she knows anything!"

Master Crowe shook his head gravely. "The woman is not exactly a friend to me, but she is hardly the only one from whom young George could have taken his lead. It is often the way of things, child. People fear most what they understand least. I am not loved by the ignorant in this town, Duffy, and it would seem that you are unpopular already, as well. Is it more than you bargained for, lad? I won't hold you to your apprenticeship if you would rather leave."

"Go back with that lot? *Bertie* doesn't even act nice anymore. Well, they can be that way if they want. Master, I am going to be an alchemist like you!" Duffy studied the old, serene face.

"Has anyone . . . do they say things to you, Master?" he asked hesitantly. "Do they call you names?"

"Call me names? Not yet. Not to my face. They fear me, I suppose, and they are not friendly, but they are not so full of fright that they forget to be polite. I expect they think I would turn the Evil Eye on them, were they rude."

It was so nearly what George Tallow had said, Duffy felt his skin prickle.

Master Crowe was stroking his beard distractedly. "And I fear it will get worse before it gets better, the way events seem to be moving. I've been doing some calculations—of course, I could be mistaken, but . . . well, come upstairs, I'd best show you."

Up into the shop they went, and after them fluttered Pajara, crooning to herself bits of the player's songs and doggerel.

Master Crowe drew open a wide, shallow drawer set in the carved wainscotting. He shuffled and searched among the parchments in it until he came upon one rather smallish sheet of vellum.

"Just so," he said with satisfaction. "Duffy, look at this, please you." He held out the page.

At the top of the leaf was a block of strange design, curls and streamers and tendrils carefully printed in black and red ink, and spattered all about with four-cornered dots. At the bottom was a picture, and very queer and frightening it was. Little men and women were running here and there, their tiny mouths open in painted screams, their arms flung up to cover their eyes, their peculiar long gowns twisted around their legs so that a few people had actually fallen down in the street. Above them, the sky was changing from blue to black as a winged beast with bloated cheeks closed its ferocious mouth around the sun.

"This picture," said Master Crowe, "was made in a land that is very far away, and it was made so long ago that the learned man who sold it to me would not even venture to guess how old it is. These lines at the top are the writing that is used in that country. Unfortunately, I cannot read them well. A foreigner, a merchant who came to Elford many years past, showed me how to read a few of the words, and he told me the story that is written here, as nearly as he could make it out."

Duffy stared at the dark colors of the illumination. In one corner, a frightened little girl was hugging the neck of a dun-colored mastiff and crying. Off to one side, unmoving, stood a grey-bearded man holding before him a golden staff. This old man, of all in the picture, was not gazing in terror at the sky or running for shelter. Instead, he was watching the people in the street. Above his head hovered a tiny, jewel-like bird—so small, it was just a few brush strokes, really. But three colors had been used by the unknown artist: green and rose and turquoise. The bird looked just like Pajara.

Master Crowe went on speaking. "It seems that, in the middle of the day, although the weather was fine and there were no storm clouds overhead, the sun went out like a guttered candle. The people believed that a demon had eaten it, bite by bite, until it was all swallowed."

Serpents that floated in golden oceans, dragons that fed on their own tails, and now monsters that devoured the very sun! Duffy began to tremble, not because of this one old picture, but because of all the dark mysteries that had closed in on his life in the last two days. He felt he was being washed away from everything familiar by that strange darkness.

"The learned ones of the kingdom, however, were not afraid," Master Crowe went on gently. "They had read in their scrolls of history and science that many times before the sun had disappeared in just such a manner. And it had always returned."

Master Crowe set down the manuscript and looked at Duffy's solemn face. "The sun is greater than any monster. It is the world's brightest star, and its warmth and light are the gift of heaven to living things here below. No demon can swallow a star, child, any more than you could swallow a candle flame. However grim you see things become, there will always be a voice to call all back from the darkness: your own voice, if none other. *If* you truly love the light."

Duffy nodded then. The picture was alarming, but his master was surely a wise man. And after all, had not this all happened very long ago? Why, only a babe would be scared now.

But Master Crowe seemed to read his thoughts. "You must trust me, child, and believe with all your heart what I have just told you, for we have a bad time ahead of us. Brave men will cower at what they behold, and many folk in Elford Town are going to doubt their senses and curse heaven, holding us to blame, I fear. I have done some mathematical figuring and consulted all the most learned books that I own. Very soon, right here in Elford, people will see the sun swallowed, just as it appears in this picture—except that they'll see no demon. Even so, folk will be terrified. But you and I must remember that we know better."

Suddenly, Pajara squawked—a loud, ungracious noise—as a shadow fell across the shop. Master Crowe and Duffy looked up, startled, to see Mistress Cotter standing in the doorway, blocking the light from outside. Silhouetted against the brightness, she looked sparer and meaner than ever, a hissing bone of a woman, sputtering like grease in a pan. The unpleasant, sulky little dog she held was yapping nastily.

"Welladay, Master Apothecary," she said. "I see you have found a familiar as low as yourself for your mysterious work. I have come to have back my money of you." She waved aside the protest she anticipated. "I saw you consorting with that outlawed beggar yestereve. Have you no respect for decent folk? Oh, you'll spend your time freely enough with vicious brats and thieving vagabonds, and all Elford knows that beggars pay you not so much as a groat for the herbs you give *them*. But honest citizens must part with outrageous amounts of their hard-earned coin for cures. And cures, what's more, that don't work as they ought. It's not to be borne! You deserve no payment from me, and I'll have it back, if you please or no."

She set down her yammering dog, who immediately commenced a frantic and noisy pursuit of Pajara as its mistress advanced toward the counter. When her scowling and angry eyes fell upon the ancient vellum, she froze in her tracks. Pajara, safely perched beyond the dog's peevish snapping, chose that unfortunate moment to display her ability to mimic what she'd heard.

"*Here in Elford,*" the bird pronounced in Djano's voice, "*I would rather see the sun swallowed.*"

Mistress Cotter gasped and clutched at her stringy throat.

"Sorcerer!" she hissed. "I've known it all along. No one but a devil would bear such willing company to a devilish old man such as you! Oh, all Elford knows about your nasty work. And now you've got this black-hearted bird from hell here in your shop, tormenting my poor puppy."

She was hoarse with accusations and venom, and Duffy could scarcely hear what she was saying, for the dog was rioting around the shop after Pajara, knocking into cabinets, making a confusion of falling things and flying fur and feathers.

Pajara balanced for a moment on the topmost shelf of the herb cupboard and breathed in Djano's rich, faraway accent, ". . . *can do turns to amaze the very sky!*" Then, a streak of emerald, she disappeared behind the baize door. The spaniel charged, yapping and whining, after her, down toward the workroom.

Duffy thought for a tithe of a second of the delicate machinery and fragile crystal vials on the shelves down there, and leapt after them. As he hit the bottom landing, he heard glass shatter. At the end of the corridor, dirty brown smoke billowed out of the workroom doorway.

Duffy whispered, "Oh, now they've done it!" and ran to snatch up Iseult's cage, for the fumes burned his eyes and his throat. His hands closed around it, but as he straightened up, the sudden move dizzied him, and he could not brace himself as he began to fall, and fall, and fall.

Chapter 11

The Cock's Egg

WHEN DUFFY OPENED HIS EYES, HE THOUGHT for a moment that the smoke was still hanging about him. That was only the dizziness, though, and the dull ache in his head. There was no smoke, no racketing dog, nor taunting bird. For that matter, there was no workshop.

He lay on his back, arms and legs cast out like the spokes of a wheel, one foot caught in a bramble bush. Overhead was nothing but blazing sky. Slowly, he pulled himself into a sitting position. The brambles had snagged a great rip in his stocking, and he had more than one stinging, red-beaded scratch on his ankle. He looked around. There was not much to see: jagged cliffs and dry, twisted thornbushes and league upon league of sand, all of it bleached nearly white in the heat, all of it dead.

The pierced tin box lay beside him. It was hot to the touch, but Duffy managed to pry it open. Iseult was there, so listless with heat that she did not so much as bare her teeth when Duffy lifted her out.

Never in his life had Duffy felt such thirst. His tongue was swollen and his lips cracked and stung when he opened them. From down in his chest up to his ears, his throat was raspy and sore. He thought that he must have been lying there unshaded for some time.

The thornbushes themselves looked parched, but Duffy knew there had to be some water about for them to have grown at all. He crawled around a bit, pulling up stones, searching for moist shadows underneath. Finally, he came upon a trickle of water oozing from a crack in the pale reddish sandstone. The water was brown and dirty-looking, and it tasted peculiar, but Duffy lapped at it for a while and felt a little better. Then he brought Iseult over to it. Her rosy muzzle twitched once or twice, but she decided to drink.

"How did I get here?" Duffy wondered aloud. "Where am I?" For surely he was nowhere near Elford Town, where the sunlight was silken and merry, and the river and all its streams and ditches greened the meadows and woods, and the very stones in the shallows grew moss as a peach grew velvet. Here the sun was a cruel and weary punishment, and the whine of a hot wind got into Duffy's head until he thought he couldn't bear it.

Was this more magic? Of course—the crash he'd heard in the workshop, the smoke. The alchemist's cellar was full of sleeping danger, and the accident had awakened it again.

Duffy felt sick, and he couldn't understand why the magic, which was supposed to be such a wonderful thing, seemed to be turning out all wrong, confusing, terrible, brutal.

He lifted Iseult onto his shoulder. That seemed cooler than carrying her in his hands. As long as he moved carefully, she seemed content to stay there. Slowly he stood up and began walking around aimlessly. There was nothing else to do. Having no idea where home was, he could think of no way to get there.

"Does Master Crowe know what has happened?" Duffy whispered into the still air. He wished now that he'd told his master about the snake in the bottle.

Dismally, he scuffed his foot into a sand dune and kicked sand into the air. Then he picked up a rock and tossed it, without marking any target first. But Iseult had to dig her claws into his neck to keep from sliding, so he didn't do that anymore. Besides, the awful heat was sapping his energy so, he was already thirsty again.

He had more trouble finding water this time, but at last discovered a pool of it puddled under a rock. Gently, he set Iseult down and dipped up a handful of the soup-warm water for her to lap from his palm, then one for himself.

"I had much better stay in one place, rather than risk being lost altogether," he warned himself aloud, needing the sound of his own voice. He did not say that it would not take many more hours in this merciless sun to finish them completely, but he thought it.

"Maybe travel will be possible after nightfall," he told Iseult. Now the sun was almost directly overhead. There was hardly enough room in his shadow for Iseult to crouch there. She watched Duffy closely and even let him stroke her fur. There was no more hissing, and Duffy wondered if they were friends now, or if it was just that the heat had sapped her natural antipathy.

The fissure beneath the stone where the water trickled was narrow, only slightly more than a hand's breadth across. Presently, thinking more of Master Crowe and the dim, cool cellar of the apothecary shop than of what he was doing, Duffy dabbled his fingers in the rivulet, and then trailed his hand back up into the crack as far as his elbow. What he touched caused him to draw it back with a sudden shock.

In the shadows was something small and doughy and covered with warty bumps, but it was something alive. Duffy crouched down to get a look.

It was a toad.

Now, Duffy had often played with toads at home; usually, he rather liked them. This toad, though, was somehow different—repulsive. It squatted by the trickling water, brown back hunched and yellowish belly bulging out between tiny front legs. The swampy gaze it turned on Duffy was decidedly unfriendly, and Duffy saw why it should be so. Away back, behind the toad, was an egg.

"Do toads lay eggs?" Duffy whispered, and couldn't remember. He thought he'd been told they just grew out of the slimy mud of the riverbank. At any rate, this was much bigger than any single toad's egg could have been, bigger even than a hen's egg. Duffy could see it set back in the dark cave, because it glowed with a red-gold light. It looked warm, but that was hardly comforting there in the blazing desert. The egg was resting on a bed of cinders, and the pit of Duffy's stomach knew that something inexplicable bound that red coal of an egg to this burnt-up land. Had some desert-loving monster nested here because this country was fierce and desolate? Or had the egg glowed there for countless ages, burning away grass that had once been soft with dew, burning good black earth into colorless dust, burning the very sun until it became mad and merciless itself?

The toad moved slightly, and Duffy edged away, his eyes riveted to the horrible egg. Suddenly he was tumbling backwards, sliding in the sand and dislodging pebbles, down the side of a shallow gravel pit.

The fall threw the breath out of him, but he wasn't badly hurt. Besides, it was a relief to be unable to see the fiery egg and its loathsome guardian.

Sitting up, he felt gingerly around the tingling corner of his bumped elbow. There was something about all this, he began to realize, that was weirdly familiar, but he couldn't put his finger on what it might be, or why he should have such an odd half-recognition of this strange place and its strange inhabitant.

Suddenly, on the other side of the gravel pit, something moved.

For a moment Duffy thought that it was merely his imagination playing tricks on him. But then it moved again: a thin trickle of sand slithering down from the rim of the pit. And then a form more substantial than sand. Sand-colored, lithe, with bright black eyes and black-tipped tail—Iseult.

She loped forward, almost within Duffy's reach and, stopping abruptly, sat up on her hind legs almost like a squirrel. Her sharp eyes peered directly into Duffy's face with a queer, knowing expression.

Duffy realized he was holding his breath, and let it out as slowly as he could. *She does like me, then!* He leaned over unbelievingly and smoothed his palm along her chestnut coat. For a moment, Duffy truly forgot all about the grim problem at hand. Iseult, who had been the nasty Stewbone, now trusted him. When she finally did move, it was only a few lengths away. Then she turned and looked back at Duffy.

Very slowly he crawled toward her, but just as he was almost close enough to reach out and touch her again, she skittered a bit farther away. Again Duffy followed, but still she stayed just out of reach. It almost seemed as if Iseult wanted him to follow her. Remembering the awful toad and the glowing egg, Duffy decided he would just as soon get moving.

"And perhaps we'll find some cleaner water, eh, girl?" he said to the stoat and stood, his elbow no longer stinging.

Iseult continued to lead, and with many a stop and start they made their way around the foot of one of the sandstone mesas.

Clearly, Iseult had some particular destination in mind. Although her gait was leisurely, it was steady and purposeful.

Do you know this desert, then?" Duffy whispered, though his head was awhirl with thoughts: *How could she? Could* he *trust* her? *What else was there to do?*

Presently they approached the foot of another red-brown cliff, and Duffy thought they would have to change direction. But there ahead, partially concealed by a dune of rippled sand, arched a wide cave-mouth. Here the stoat finally paused and did not move on.

At first sight, Duffy had thought the cave a mere hollow dug by the wind that constantly scraped across the cliff face. Now he realized it was a large cavern. As he stepped under the sheltering overhang of stone, he had a sudden eerie feeling of being watched. Apprehensively he glanced around.

What he had at first taken for natural markings on the rock, he now saw, was the work of long-gone painters. Like Master Wing's parchment, these were pictures to be read: faded, crumbling friezes of animals and hunters who galloped in herds or ran by twos and threes, antlers or bows and spears outthrust before them. Here were straight-horned stags in nervous flight; here, heavy-shouldered bulls bristling with the hunters' shafts, and long-necked camelopards fleeing absurdly on their stilt legs. And the tiny men pursuing—how gaunt and lean, how desperately hungry they must be, to run, hearts bursting, after those fleet hooves and fierce horns.

Duffy's eyes traveled in amazement across the stone pictures. Then, with a shock that left him weak, his glance fell across a painting of another beast. It was monstrous; it chilled his blood. And he knew that he recognized it. Master Crowe had told him about it the night before, but he had been so tired, he had not been attending properly. What had the apothecary said? Something about its eye. Eye—yes!

"If it turns its eye upon a thing, or breathes upon it, that thing is blasted. Living things it turns to stone." What else? *"It is the King Serpent, and some say a toad hatches it from an egg laid by a cock, and we call it a cockatrice."* So! He'd remembered.

He stared dumbly at the rock painting. There was the egg, a jagged crack running across it, and the immense form of a serpent rearing up from it.

Duffy felt the suck of panic, felt himself being drawn back toward that other serpent, that other boundless horror, not of burning heat, but of timeless water. That one, though, had been floating in death. Even looking at this crudely painted image, Duffy realized that this serpent was taut with ferocious life. Behind its beaked head flared a great pair of straining wings. It had a comb very like a crown.

"I must be brave," he whispered, and the cave sent back his words, but nevertheless he was shaking.

"Surely, if my heart is stout, courage will save me," he told himself. But his heart beat against his ribs like a caged wild bird, for the thought he could not keep away battered at him: *What use is all the courage in the world against a monster who has only to look upon one to turn flesh and blood to stone, and to shatter one's bones like Venice glass?*

Then a calming thought dawned in Duffy's mind. He was *not* alone. Not entirely. There was Iseult. She had brought him to this place—as if she had known exactly where to find it.

"Surely," he whispered, "surely that means something." Then he left the cave.

The stoat was sitting on a low ridge of crumbled rock, looking back toward the cliffs that hid the toad's nest. Duffy moved toward her, confused, but when his stunted shadow fell across the ridge, she leapt away. And when Duffy tried once more to come near, Iseult turned with a hiss that bared her needle-sharp teeth.

Then suddenly she ran away, across the desert, her long back gathering up and stretching out in a queer, sinuous motion that covered ground with surprising swiftness.

A great blast shook the earth, and hurtling stones and sand filled the air. Duffy knew—even without seeing it—what had happened.

The egg had hatched.

CHAPTER 12

ISEULT AND THE COCKATRICE

UFFY STOOD PETRIFIED AND STARED BACK AT the cliff. It had been solid, an unremarkable fact of the land. Now it shivered like the shoulders of a great animal awakening, and torrents of dirt and boulders poured down its sides. The earth all around was shaking, heaving, retching itself open in great fissures. From beyond the cliff came the roar of exploding stone: mesas shattering like pottery. And toward the cause of it all the tiny stoat was running madly.

"Stop!" Duffy cried, "It'll kill you!" But the wind whipped the words out of his mouth, and they were gone.

Iseult did not hear. Duffy thought numbly that he must catch her, and somehow he lifted his feet and stumbled forward, trying to run fast enough to get to her in time. But his steps caught in the sand, and when a small piece of flying rock hit his chest, he went down. Struggling to his knees, he looked after the stoat in desperation. He couldn't even see her among the windblown dunes.

He huddled on the ground in terror. The air, already harsh and restless, now tore furiously across the scorched earth—beaten, he knew, by immense wings. The sky roared.

Duffy's hands tried to block out the sounds of the destruction, but to no avail. Dirt fell on him as if it were rain, and again and again he was hit by flying shards of the blasted cliffs. He stared dumbly at the rocks as they fell, sending up geysers of dust where they hit the ground.

Iseult had been running so fast. . . . Could there be any hope she was not already dead?

Overhead, something hovered like a vulture, tossing erratically on the currents of turbulent, dust-clogged air. Then, in slow and menacing arcs, it began to sink, and Duffy could make out what it was—a single, smoking, bronze-colored feather. It was bigger than Duffy, bigger than a grown man, much bigger than a silken-coated, bright-eyed stoat.

Duffy staggered to his feet and moved forward again, shielding his eyes against the sand, fighting his way into the hot wind. Iseult had been headed around the left shoulder of the cliff when he'd lost sight of her, and now he bent his own steps that way. The landslides had dumped a new spur of rubble at the foot of the cliff. The grit, rather than settling, was swirling and foaming in rust-colored whirlwinds. Duffy flung himself down behind one of the boulders. His lungs were raw with the effort of breathing, and now he needed a moment to collect his wits.

But where was the moment to come from?

And what had become of Iseult?

He pushed himself up across the boulder and, gasping, beheld the cockatrice.

It was all wind and fire, too enormous to be animal, too furious to be anything else. It moved convulsively, like a fighting cock, strutting and swaggering on its two spurred, scaly legs, beating its black-cloud wings and slewing its python tail. A serpentine neck, hackled with feathers, whipped back and forth close to the ground, raising so much dust Duffy could not clearly see its head. Nor did he want to see it. The cockatrice was an unnatural thing, neither fowl nor viper, as wretched as it was terrible, as horrible to his sense as to his senses.

The long neck darted along the rocky strew, and Duffy could see fountains of gravel leaping up wherever the monster's glance fell. He knew that, should it look toward him, there would be no more Elford or Master Crowe to think of, no more magic beyond the nightmare accident that had set him here, helpless, in the desert.

If it turns its eye upon a thing, or breathes upon it, that thing is blasted.

His hands were scraped bloody from the work of crossing that waste, from falling and scrambling. Now he clutched at the broken rock where he balanced, his knuckles tight and white. Fear was like a fever. His whole body trembled with it.

Suddenly, there was a scarlet flash, low over the ground. For a second, Duffy saw the tyrant comb of the cockatrice as it snapped to the strike. Then the whine of the wind was drowned in a new sound.

It was a hiss. It was a crow. It rent the sky as if it were the flaming trumpet on the Day of Judgment. It rose higher and higher until, with a sudden strangled spasm, it ceased.

As Duffy watched, the monster folded and buckled like a tower collapsing, and fell silently toward the earth.

That silence was so startling that, for a moment, it seemed more deafening than all that had gone before. Then the crash shook the ground, a moment of sound before the earth was still again. Even the wind seemed to be dying into a desultory breeze. And though Duffy had not cried for fear, now, in his relief, he felt tears spilling down his cheeks. For a minute he thought he would throw up, but that passed. He leaned his head against his folded arms and sobbed.

After a while, when the tears became fewer, Duffy began to wonder what had actually happened, but he could not think, only stare ahead.

Perhaps it was only imagination, but the sunlight did not seem quite so brazen now. And as he looked around him, Duffy thought he saw subtle changes coming over the wasteland. Some of the scrubby bushes showed a faint tinge of yellowy green along their crooked stems, like willows almost ready to leaf. It was as if, while Duffy was crying, the sap had begun running again, through the parched earth and right up into the few little plants that had managed to hold on through the long drought.

He felt a twinge of hope that now he might even find a way to get back to Elford, back to Master Crowe.

But when he finally scrambled over the rocks, all such thoughts were suddenly driven away. Before him was an awful scene.

There lay the body of the cockatrice, immense, glistering, like some strange mountain newly heaved up out of the earth's bowels. Its enormous feathers clumped unpreened where death had left them: copper red across the breast, speckled with gold on the back and wings, blue-green where the serpent's tail arched away like a cock's plume. Between the pale, film-lidded eyes, Duffy could see a small wound.

Was that what killed it, then? he wondered. But he had seen no one deal the blow. Where was the hero?

Just behind the monster's head, a new spring was bubbling out of the sand, and from its verges a veil of greenery was spreading out in all directions. Blades of grass, tendrils of vine—they came up so quickly, Duffy could almost see them grow. Already, dust was blowing over the huge carcass, clinging to its curves, hiding it. Soon there would be nothing but a softly rolling hill rising above the spring.

Yet Duffy could feel nothing but sorrow and confusion. He was all alone in this strange world. Even Iseult was gone. And for what madness? To go rushing toward the cockatrice and the explosions.

Just then, Duffy caught sight of a tiny patch of pale sand that was not turning green, although moss had crept all around it.

With a cry of joy, he ran forward.

"Iseult!" he cried.

Abruptly the exultant cry froze on his lips.

It *was* Iseult, and by some miracle she was alive. But who would have known this limp, dull-eyed creature for the bright and engaging animal she had been? The sand-colored fur had turned ash white. It was mussed and peaky, and dust caked around a crimson gash that ran down one flank.

Now, too late, Duffy knew the reason for the hissing and snarling. Iseult had not only warned him about the cockatrice, she had also led him out of harm's way and kept him from going back where he would surely have been killed. And now, she herself would die unless he could do something for her.

Gently he lifted her and smoothed the ruffled fur. He could feel the muscles around the wound knotted agonizingly—spasms caused by cockatrice venom, he was sure.

As tenderly as he knew how, Duffy carried Iseult over to the spring and began to bathe the blood and dirt away, while he ransacked his memory for the scraps of lore Master Crowe had taught him in the two days they'd gone about their work. Cradling the little beast, Duffy stared at the rippling surface of the water, trying to recall all the rhymes he'd memorized to help him learn healing. His face screwed up with concentration. In the shop, he had muttered verse after verse, proud of how much he'd learned in so short a time. But now his wisdom seemed piteously small and scattered.

"*Centaury cools fever. Poppy brings sleep. Foxglove the failing heart will keep. Coltsfoot for cough and chill of damp. . . .*"

What was the next line? Somehow, Duffy was sure it was exactly what he needed to undo the mischief of the cockatrice's poison. Distractedly, he watched the twists of water bubbling up through the pool and spreading into ring after ring across the silvery surface. *Campion? Loosestrife? Black medick?* Under the water, ripples came together in ever-changing shapes, and colors that shimmered and fled. Duffy stretched his mind as far as he could, hearing Master Crowe's voice in his mind. *Asafoetida? Garlic? Rue?*

Rue!

As he thought it, the ripples, the shapes and colors whirled and came together, and through the shifting waters he saw Master Crowe's face, the eyes rayed about with wrinkles, the lips forming words: "Duffy, where are you, child?"

Other words hummed and spun in Duffy's brain: *"Foul oil of rue for the sinew's cramp. . . ."*

Holding Iseult tightly against him, Duffy stepped into the water and found himself back in the apothecary's cellar.

CHAPTER 13

TO REMEDY A POISON

HOURS BEFORE, WHEN DUFFY HAD RUN DOWN the stairs after Mistress Cotter's dog, Master Crowe had stayed in the shop trying vainly to soothe the woman's noisy anger. All he could say had not calmed her perceptibly. But when the bedraggled spaniel had slunk whining back into the room, she had at least taken her scolding out of earshot.

"You have not heard the last of me," she warned as she stalked out. Crowe had been only too sure she spoke the truth. She would certainly tell her story far and wide, convincing people he was courting doom for Elford Town. There was bound to be trouble.

Crowe had shaken his head and gone downstairs.

The cellar was a disheartening mess of overturned equipment, puddled liquids, and ruined powders. Fortunately, nothing important had been destroyed, for he kept the rarest stock of roots and balms that had to be bought from foreign travelers on the topmost shelves, tightly closed in tin boxes to discourage the rats.

Pajara was gorging herself on spilled millet. Duffy was nowhere to be found, but Crowe had assumed he had gone to the river to fetch water for mopping. After fishing out of the wreckage one or two of the more delicate pieces of machinery, Crowe went back up to the shop and began to mix a tonic for Master Jarrett.

Few customers had come to the door that morning. When the quinsy medicine was done, and a batch for stomachache as well, it occurred to the old man that Duffy was taking an unduly long time with the mopping. He went downstairs to see if anything were amiss.

The workshop was just as he had last seen it. Nothing had been mopped at all and there was still no sign of Duffy.

Uneasily, Crowe remembered Duffy's vexing encounter by the river that morning, and a chilly intuition swept up his spine: Duffy was in danger.

Surely Mistress Cotter could not have stirred the whole town so quickly, he thought, *and in any event, I myself would have been the first target.* "Yet," he muttered, "were the child to walk unwittingly into the midst of those suspicious gossips down among the turnip and onion heaps in the market square, might they not detain him? He would surely seem the best source of intelligence regarding me." He shook his head at the thought.

Taking his cloak, Crowe closed the shop door and went out into the alleys. There was no one in sight on the riverbank, and no sign that anything out of the ordinary had happened there. He turned his back on the water lapping at the muddy landing, and started into the streets of Elford.

Up and down he walked, asking in the Guild Square and Milk Close and Silver Street, but no one acknowledged having seen a slim boy in a greyish jerkin.

In Fish Lane, two ragamuffins threw oyster shells after him, but without animosity. They would have done the same to any stranger.

At the center of town, there were doubtful looks and whispers, and no one would speak to Crowe at all. His knock at the almshouse gate went unanswered.

Nor was Mistress Cotter in evidence. Although Crowe supposed she could be at the magistrate's house making a complaint, he began to hope her anger had been distracted after all. Sighing aloud, he went back home to his cellar, half expecting to find Duffy already safely returned.

The cellar was empty except for Pajara. She perched on the dwarf skeleton, preening her wing feathers and cackling, "*Vicious brats and thieving stage monkeys.*" She sounded just like Mistress Cotter.

Master Crowe sighed.

It had been several hours now since Duffy had disappeared. Perhaps, all said and done, he had been frightened by Mistress Cotter's accusations and had believed them. Or perhaps he simply did not want to be apprenticed to so unpopular a master. With trouble and danger afoot, perhaps it were better so.

Master Crowe took off his cloak and began to clean up the mess on the floor.

"Would that one of your four languages could say where the boy is gone," he said to the parrot. Pajara fluttered over to sit on his shoulder.

Suddenly, the air around the two stirred. Crowe turned. The back gate was closed, as he had left it. The warm breeze seemingly came from nowhere. And then words: a boy's voice.

"*Centaury cools fever. Poppy brings sleep. . . .*"

It was Duffy's voice, reciting a healing verse. Hiding, probably, up to some prank. But the voice was not coming out of a shadowy corner. And, Crowe reminded himself, he had not thought Duffy the kind to play such inconsiderate games.

Uncertainly, he looked around.

"Are my old ears playing me tricks? The voice is just at my elbow!"

He stepped backward a few paces and felt chilly. Where he had been standing, the air shimmered dizzily. In a hot summer courtyard, air wavered like that, or before the alchemical athanor when the fire inside was roaring. In a damp, cool cellar, the sight was eerie.

"Duffy," he entreated, "where are you, child?"

Suddenly, Duffy was before him.

Master Crowe's lined face mirrored his astonishment. Where there had been only stale air and dust motes, now stood a sunburnt apprentice with something small clutched to his jerkin.

Duffy knew he owed the old man an explanation, but his thoughts were whirling.

"Rue, Master—have you any rue?" he gasped. "She will die if we aren't quick."

"She? Who? Duffy, where have you been?"

Unable to answer, Duffy shook his head and held out Iseult for Master Crowe's questioning eyes. Crowe's glance took in the wound and the blackish poison oozing from it. Years of experience told him there was no time to waste.

"Rue, you say? Yes, of course, rue . . . muscular spasms, no doubt some paralysis . . . powdered, do we want, or oil?"

The rusty gown flapped hastily from shelf to shelf. "Leaves, I think. Perhaps she can eat them. Some oil to put on the cut place, as well."

" 'Tisn't bleeding much now," Duffy said anxiously.

"Crusting over, is it? A baleful sign. The corruption will not drain out of the body unless the wound remains open for a bit. Perhaps a poultice would help. Here, though—here is fresh rue. Will she open her mouth?"

Duffy held the wilted, frilly stem before Iseult's muzzle, but she did not respond to the scent, nor even open her eyes.

"We shall have to pry it open, then," said Master Crowe. Fetching a blunt silver bodkin, he gently forced the clenched jaws apart.

Duffy placed a scrap of rue in Iseult's mouth and waited, his heart hammering in his ears. Secretly he feared it was all too late. The stoat had not moved for a very long time.

But then the teeth closed and, ever so feebly, chewed on the herb, some instinct for preservation proving stronger than the poison. When Duffy held another sprig under the black nose, Iseult accepted it without any need for the bodkin.

Master Crowe mixed a poultice of meal and oil of rue and, first wiping away the troublesome scab, applied the healing mess to the wound.

"Now, if she is kept warm—well, I make no promises, for I never saw such thick venom, but I think she will recover. Child, what are you doing?"

Duffy was making to secure Iseult in the bosom of his shirt. "Will it not keep her warm, sir, to hold her so?" he asked timidly.

"No doubt, but so would a bit of fleece, and the fleece would not jar her by moving about under her," Crowe said gravely. "Duffy, 'tis well meant, I can see, but where did you get the creature, and why are you at such pains to preserve it? There is more to this than simple charity to dumb beasts, I think. And there is another matter, as well, for surely you did not *walk* into this room."

Duffy thought fast. The old man did not look angry; yet for a sickening moment, Duffy remembered what could happen to him if his master should think him mad. Even if he weren't actually locked up for a lunatic, he surely would have to go back to the almshouse. He thought of Master Humphrey, who had almost sold him to Mistress Cotter, of George Tallow bullying the little boys, of Hugh and Bertie crying themselves to sleep at night. He thought of Pajara chirping drowsily on her perch the evening before, comfortably at home after only a few hours, and of Iseult imprisoned in a box and forced to be mean and nasty if she were ever to get anything to eat. But still, he *had* stolen her. What would Crowe think about that? Would he understand? Would he make Duffy give up Iseult even so? Like the balance scales upstairs in the shop, Duffy's heart lurched up and down.

Master Crowe was waiting for an answer.

Mute and miserable, Duffy looked down at his feet. There, clinging to one heel, was a great, downy bit of bronze-colored feather. Duffy tried to hide it with his other foot, then reached down to snatch it behind his back. But the stooping jostled Iseult so she whimpered, and the feather—still warm—seemed to strain at his hand like a bent-over sapling.

It was altogether too much. Master Humphrey had given his age as eleven, but Duffy was nowhere near so old yet. And Hugh and Bertie had not been the only ones who sometimes cried at night. Tears filled his eyes and spilled over. With his free hand, he held Iseult out to Master Crowe, so that the saltwater wouldn't fall on her wound. Then, with an earnest but largely unsuccessful attempt to stifle his sobs, he told his master all that happened, all that he had done.

CHAPTER 14

NO STARLING'S WING, NO PEACOCK'S FAN

I WENT DOWN THE STAIRS, AND THERE WAS brown smoke . . . ," he began.

From beginning to end, it took surprisingly little time to tell, though Duffy's voice faltered several times at the memory of this or that moment of horror. And the feather clutched behind him seemed to be growing warmer and warmer every second.

Master Crowe neither grew angry nor laughed at him, nor did he look doubtful. He settled Iseult in a fleece-lined box, on a warm shelf. Then he sat stroking his beard, listening carefully and, to Duffy's great relief, appearing to believe the incredible tale.

Just as he finished his story, Duffy gasped and dropped the hot, brazen bit of feather on the worktable, next to the silver bodkin.

It must have been one of the downy breast feathers, for it was only the size of Duffy's hand. Yet it was a miracle of wild and subtle color, hues shifting rebelliously from cinnabar to garnet to darkest Tyrian. No starling's wing ever shimmered so; indeed, no peacock's fan ever radiated such live heat.

Master Crowe gazed upon it, and his face lit at a stroke with the wonder he had been carefully resisting.

"Then it was no delirium," he said at last. "Duffy, with all the worry, I thought my eyes might have deceived me. But *you have gone into some other world*. And brought back . . . *this!*"

"Master," Duffy pleaded, "I did not mean to leave. I was not trying to bring it back here."

But Crowe seemed to find this more wonderful still. "Truly, you were born to be an alchemist. I am honored to have such an apprentice." He nodded. "There is magic in you, but also providence. You could not know such lore, but the feather of a cockatrice is reputed to be of much virtue in alchemy. All unwitting, you have brought one back."

"Nothing like this ever happened before I came here," Duffy said with a whimper. "I don't want things like this to happen. What if Mistress Cotter finds out? What if Iseult doesn't get better? I don't understand all these magic attacks."

"Not '*attacks*,' " Master Crowe said slowly. "Doorways. Doorways opening. This is a clear omen. We must try for the Stone today. The art comes naturally to you now. It is in your bones, and in your blood, and in your heart." Seeing Duffy's protesting face, he laughed almost lightly and added, "And in your feet also, it would seem. What we shall learn!"

Duffy looked at his master, perplexed.

"Sir," he stammered, "I don't know about my feet. . . ." He glanced down at them as he spoke, as if they were strangers he hardly recognized. "But it is still a puzzle to my head. The monster, the . . . what you call the cockatrice—*and* the dead snake, when it got big—what do *they* have to do with alchemist experiments? They were *real*. They were horrible! You wouldn't *think* of experiments if they were around—begging your pardon, sir, but it's *true!* They were *huge*. They were *dangerous*."

"And alchemy is so safe and tidy." Master Crowe shook his

head, his eyebrows drawn together, a funny expression on his face. "Understand, I do not say you will not make mistakes, nor that I've any more courage or presence of mind than you, my boy—indeed, your innocence may be your best protection. But 'tis *all* magic, Duffy, and it all follows laws of magic—just as surely and precisely as the stars keep within the laws of the heavens.

"Now, we have much work to do."

Gingerly he lifted the trembling cockatrice feather and set it on a heavy plate, covering it with a glass dome to prevent its blowing haphazardly around the workroom.

"What of Mistress Cotter?" asked Duffy. "What of George? You *know* they'll make trouble."

Master Crowe shrugged, his eyes steady. "We will deal with them and the rest of the citizenry when we see what they come to bargain with. Now, though, we must not put off our greatest task. We must put aside any business that is not healing, and act as alchemists. This is where we'll find our own best courage, after all."

"Then the Philosophers' Stone is a charm for courage?" Duffy inquired hopefully.

Crowe began to clear the table, in which task Duffy joined him unbidden.

"Say, rather, 'tis the Key Charm," Master Crowe said. " 'Tis all a code, you see, a secret cipher, everything we do. Oh, there are those who call themselves alchemists because they melt all sorts of things and puff on their bellows day and night. No doubt some of the puffers learn a great deal about smelting and smithery. But when *true* alchemists say 'mercury,' they do not mean merely a little bit of quicksilver. They mean, something *in themselves* that is quick and bright. That silvery liquid in that vial that stands on the first shelf, next to Iseult, Duffy, that is mercury. Bring it over, if you please."

Duffy hurried to do his bidding, returned with the vial, then settled on a stool.

"When we alchemists say we will take a lump of lead and add other substances and so make gold," Crowe continued, starting to pace, "we mean that we will take the dull and ugly in this life and show it new thoughts and feelings, so we will be changed in substance and soul into something beautiful."

"I was just waiting for Iseult to trust me," Duffy said simply. "Even at the almshouse, when George Tallow wasn't around." Then, hearing his own words, he realized something more. "I was waiting to get away from Master Humphrey. I was always thinking of doing things I thought I'd like better. Trying to change. Is that lead into gold?"

Master Crowe nodded. Then, with a gesture that took in the workroom and all its equipment, he added, "All of this is exercise for our minds. Also, for our spirits and our souls. And why? Because: *As it is above, so below.* Not everyone *has* magic and luck such as yours. But every heart has dreams, and everyone has a mind and a will to turn toward the truth—as a plant turns to face the sun."

Duffy felt a great weight had been placed on his shoulders. "I'm from the almshouse. How can I learn it all?" he said.

Crowe regarded him with tenderness. "A rich diet for a half-starved creature, eh? Well, you are already changing, child. To find the Philosophers' Stone *you* must become the Philosopher—the lover of wisdom. They say the Stone is the keystone of your own heart and soul."

Master Crowe had been pacing around the room as he spoke. Now he settled himself again on a stool like the one on which Duffy was sitting.

"My own teachers, many years ago, taught me to mix this and that, and to burn it all to ash, and then to dissolve it. Those are the first steps toward making the Stone. Shall we begin?"

It was a solemn moment.

"Yes," said Duffy at last. And then, "I hope it works."

"Well, then: let us say this lead is Crowe, an old man, grave and dented by his years. This mercury, quick and bright, like an apprentice, comes to join him. . . ."

CHAPTER 15

THAT WHICH MAKES THE JEWEL

M I THE MERCURY, THEN?" DUFFY ASKED, pleased.

"Indeed you are. Since you have come, I must try to remember how I thought as a child, in order to speak so you can understand. This is a gift you give me. I am already changed by you."

The master changed by the apprentice! This was a novel thought, but one that Duffy would have to consider later, for Crowe went on speaking as he measured off a bit of quicksilver and splashed it in entrancing globules into the crucible, which already held the ball of lead.

"What else shall we say has changed us since you arrived?"

"The serpent," Duffy answered promptly, "for one thing. Nothing like that ever happened before."

Master Crowe went to the shelf and drew off a spoonful or so of the liquor from the serpent's bottle and set the measure next to the experimental flask.

"Now, what of our friend Wing? Duffy, call him to mind and tell me—what color shall his ingredient have?"

Duffy closed his eyes and thought of the incensed room in Devil's Own. Master Wing himself was a pale ochre color, like old ivory, but that didn't seem quite what Master Crowe was asking. Duffy opened his eyes.

"Dark blue?" he asked. "That's what he chooses to wear. At least, when I saw him he was wearing it."

Crowe signed thoughtful approval, pointing to a chunk of dark blue rock on the floor in one corner of the cellar. Duffy hefted it and brought it over.

"I believe this is a Persian ore," the old alchemist remarked as he chipped off an almond-sized nugget and pulverized it with a small hammer. Powdered, the stone looked a tarnished grey.

Duffy had been considering the next ingredient. He had all sorts of ideas but none seemed just right, until—"Master, if feathers are good to use, what of Pajara's? She lost some when the dog was after her."

Crowe gave him a sharp look. "An interesting idea, my boy. I would not have thought of it, myself. But why not?" He paused a moment, thoughtful. Then, resolutely, "Yes. Yes. Did not Djano tell us he once changed gold into bird? Perhaps we can change a bit back, by and by, eh?"

Duffy ran upstairs and came back with a greeny tuft of down.

"I can't think of anything to put in for George," Duffy worried. "No color seems really right, and I don't have anything of his . . . I mean, Iseult isn't *his,* is she, she's her own . . ." Duffy's words petered out.

Master Crowe knit his brows. "She has put the cockatrice feather at our disposal, that is sufficient for her, I should hope!" He laughed suddenly. "Didn't you say George's name is Tallow?"

Duffy laughed, too, and fetched a candle stub. Master Crowe pared off a few curls of the tan tallow and set them beside the crucible.

"Worse fortune, I suppose we must add something for our neighbor, Mistress Cotter."

"I know the very stuff!" Duffy said triumphantly. "You were using it yesterday for the soap to mop away evil humors." He clambered up the shelves and took down a clay jar full of a stinking yellowish powder. "It smells like rotten eggs."

Crowe smiled at his apprentice, but his eyes had become a trifle awed. "This is an important ingredient, Duffy, which you have selected. Essential, I would say. How you knew . . ." Then he seemed to shake off his sudden concern.

"Most exciting, most intriguing of all—the plume of the fallen beast." Ceremoniously, Crowe removed the glass dome that had covered the cockatrice feather, took up a razor-sharp knife, and trimmed one barb. "It warms my hands so," he remarked, "the joints pretend they're young." He placed the red next to Pajara's green on a burnished copper dish, securing the rest of the feather reverently in a glass jar.

"Now," said Master Crowe, and the cellar grew very quiet. He reached for Duffy's hand just as Duffy was holding his own hand out, and gave it a squeeze. "The athanor is heated, I believe." He took up a pair of tongs and opened the tightly fitted door of a curious, house-shaped little oven. With two fingers, he sprinkled the iron plate above the coals with a few drops of water. They skittered and disappeared. Crowe closed the athanor and carefully scraped the greyish blue rock powder into the crucible.

"Now, Duffy, you must add as much of the yellow sulfur as we added quicksilver."

Carefully, holding his breath, Duffy did as he was instructed.

"And the tallow. And the lead. Good. Remember the order of these operations." Using the tongs again, Crowe opened the athanor and set the crucible inside. As he turned the latch, he said, "Press two fingers against the stripes of your wrist and tell me when you've counted eight-and-seventy."

In the silence that followed, Pajara sailed across the workroom and landed on Duffy's shoulder. So great was his concentration, though, he did not lose count.

"Seventy-eight," he said aloud, and Crowe pulled open the tiled door of the alchemical oven.

In the crucible, all had melted, but not all parts had blended. On one side was a silvery puddle, on the other a yellowish liquid. Between them was a rivulet of wax.

Master Crowe took up a long glass wand and stirred the whole into one, whereupon it all turned black. "There's your Ethiopian Sea," he nodded, apparently satisfied with the work so far. "Now introduce the green tint," he added, holding the wand toward Duffy.

Duffy touched the tip of the stirring rod to the green feather as Crowe muttered, "The gift of Pajara, lovely as the moon."

Looking briefly at his master, Duffy submerged the tiny feather in the blackness within the crucible. Crowe closed the athanor and this time he himself counted silently, nodding his head gently with each number.

"Eight-and-seventy . . . ah yes, yes indeed. What marvel. Duffy, look at that!" Duffy thought his heart was about to fly out the top of his head. Even Crowe could hardly contain his excitement.

The mixture in the athanor had become a brilliant April green, touched with rainbows where the light of the furnace lay on its surface.

"Heaven help us, we will surely make the Jewel this time," Crowe said. Gently he poured the measure of amber liquor directly into the crucible, so not a drop ran down the side.

"The red, now, child. Now!"

The fragment of cockatrice feather clung for a second to the end of the wand. Then Duffy tapped it, ever so lightly, on the lip of the crucible, and the feather drifted loose and began to sink toward the iridescent greenness below.

Crowe closed the athanor and counted slowly, out loud, to twenty-two.

When he opened the door of the radiant little house once more, the green had gone all white as snow, and the feather was just coming to rest.

Duffy gasped.

The feather seemed to draw all the whiteness to itself in one rush, the particles shooting into frostlike fronds, layer within sudden layer, solidifying, curling around one another, crystalliz-ing. For one breathless moment, Master Crowe and Duffy his apprentice beheld in their crucible a gleaming jewel, clear as ice, filled with fire.

Then a puff of golden mist streamed from the heart of the Stone, filling the crucible. The cloud twinkled with a brightness almost impossible to look upon—then it was gone.

The sound it made when it disappeared was like an apple hit-ting the ground on a dew-wet morning.

The crucible was absolutely empty.

CHAPTER 16

THE BULLY, THE BIRD, AND MASTER BUCK

E DID IT!” DUFFY WHISPERED, AWED. “BUT where did it go? Why didn’t it last?”

Master Crowe looked dazed. He shook his head. “I do not know.” He reached for the stirring rod, then let it lie. There was nothing left to stir, no ashes to poke through, no thinnest residue remaining in the curve of the cooling glass or inside the athanor.

“Some detail was wrong. Our attention was not perfect for making it durable, only for making it. The fire, the timing . . .” He paused, hands folded around wrists within his cavernous sleeves. An expression of doubt played across his features. “Some bitterness in our hearts, I fear—some bit of fear, itself.”

He shook his head again, then, and a smile grew into his look. “But we did have it, Duffy, right here. That we did. The Philosophers’ Stone. The Jewel of Life. What matter where it went? Where it is now, blessings there. The great thing is, Duffy, we have seen it.”

How strange, Duffy was thinking, to feel such loss and such joy together. For he also was one great smile now, the delight racing in his very blood.

"It's beautiful!" he shouted. "It's the most wonderful thing ever!"

Crowe paced the workroom, excited. "This is not in any record I have seen, that the Stone comes into sight and then vanishes. And yet—why not? They speak of its indestructability. Is not Life both visible and invisible? I must read more deeply in the works of the old teachers. I must ask Wing if he has ever heard—"

He did not finish his sentence. There was a sudden thud upstairs in the shop, as if someone were up there—another muffled thump, and the crash of splintering wood.

Duffy was the first to react. As he charged up the stairs, the thumps and crashes continued. When he came into the room, he saw that the shop had been broken into, and a sorry scene it was. The drawers of the herb cabinet had been smashed to kindling, and the carefully gathered and labeled medicines had been dumped in heaps on the rush-matted floor. The leather-covered money box lay empty in a pile of crumbled anise twigs, like a broken egg in a raided nest. In the middle of the room crouched George Tallow, his back toward the stairs, sucking a bleeding finger and struggling to hold onto a canvas sack that twitched and bumped around like a thing possessed.

"Hell spawn! Bite *me*, will you?" he was snarling. "I'll wring your neck—see if I don't." He hadn't heard Duffy enter.

For once, Duffy had the advantage, and he was not slow to seize it. With a cry of rage, he leapt on George from behind and began boxing him about the ears and shoulders, yelling all the while.

"You big bully! Give that money back, you dog-nosed thief." It was a successful ambush. Though Duffy had no time to realize it, it was exhilarating, for a change, to be punching and pummeling without getting punched and pummeled back. At that moment, he was not even afraid of George.

Unfortunately, his triumph didn't last long, for the bigger lad had gotten a good grip on his sack at last. He straightened up abruptly and, peeling Duffy off his back with a sneer, sent him sprawling. Duffy was so angry, he hardly noticed that his nose was bleeding.

"Call *me* names, will you, whey-faced puppy?" George laughed disagreeably. "Call *me* a thief, eh? Where's my stoat, then? You think I'm here on my own hook? Well, I'm not. I'm here for old Cotter, too. My new mistress, I mean. I heard her talking. Your old weed-puller cheated her and said he'd put the magic on her, too. I just come to get back her money and my stoat, and there ain't no one in this here town'll say I ain't got the right to do it. I'm not afeared of him, nor of you, I'm not. I told you this morning Elford's not a town to tolerate witches and suchlike. Nor your heathen bird, neither."

He laughed again—an ugly, gurgling sound—and Duffy realized with a start that Pajara had been in the cellar when he and Crowe were tending to Iseult, and during the experiment, but not afterwards.

"You see what I do to this brute, and then maybe you'll be smart and clear out before I do the same to you—or the hangman does!"

So saying, he reached into the sack. If Duffy had been less frightened, he would have noticed the difference between George's swaggering speech and the nervous caution with which he attempted to pull Pajara out of the bag. His caution did him no good, however, for Pajara bit him again anyway.

George howled. "Blast you, I *will* wring your neck, for sure. . . ."

"Harm the bird, if you dare, and you shall regret it sorely." Master Crowe stood in the doorway, anger flashing in his eyes like heat lightning. "Twice today you have injured my apprentice, though he is smaller than you. The stoat was half-starved—do you think I couldn't see that? Now you break in here and threaten a harmless creature who has only tried to protect herself against your cruelty. Leave this house, George Tallow, and never come again." He looked George up and down, seemingly taking his measure for some purpose, and then added deliberately, "Unless you are prepared to spend the rest of your days as a toad!"

George's face went ashen. His eyes twitched from Master Crowe's face to Duffy's and back again several times as he backed toward the street door. His nerveless fingers finally dropped the canvas bag at the threshold and he turned and ran.

Pajara, newly frightened by being so roughly thumped on the floor slates, squawked and screamed in Spanish, and fought her way out of the sack at last. So panicked was she that, instead of bringing her indignation into the shop for Master Crowe to soothe, she shot outside: a flash of green against the sky, and then gone.

Duffy licked a trickle of blood off his upper lip and stood up, eyeing Master Crowe carefully. Now that the anger was waning from his old face, the apothecary looked the same as always, but Duffy felt a bit queer in his stomach.

"Would you really do it, Master?" he asked timidly. "Turn him into a toad, I mean." Duffy did not like George Tallow, but after all, he *had* known him a long time. It would be strange to see him as a toad.

Master Crowe sighed. "I almost wish I could," he said, and his voice sounded tired, very tired, and very old. "But I can't. Nor can any alchemist I ever heard of." He sighed again. "Our pretty bird is gone—I wonder if she can take care of herself here? Her own country was very different, I should think." He shook his head. "But I should have held my temper. It was a foolish threat I made, and we'll hear of it again, if I know the people of Elford." He rummaged a bit, then came over and dabbed at Duffy's nose with a witch hazel compress.

Another disconcerting thought suddenly occurred to Duffy. "He didn't drop the money."

Crowe nodded dejectedly. "Perhaps it's for the best. Perhaps it is fair. We *do* have the stoat. And if the fellow gives Mistress Cotter a few pieces of silver, her malice may cool enough to keep us out of gaol. If anyone other than our friend George heard me make that threat, I suppose I shall be held responsible for every wart in town." He straightened his back a whit. "We'd best clear away here and set to rights what we can. Things are going badly enough, but if we have no plan by the time the sun is eclipsed—for I'm sure it will be soon—we shall be in danger of a worse sort than this. We must open our shutters as soon as may be, and perhaps we can put things back to normal somehow."

It was no easy task, tidying up the wreckage George had left behind him. Only three drawers of the big cabinet had escaped unharmed, and all too many bundles of precious herbs had been ground underfoot until they were unusable.

Duffy scooped up all that was not utterly dusty, and Master Crowe sorted the heaps, for he needed no labels to recognize the scent of comfrey or the shape of rampion roots. By pulling out the last splinters of wood left in the drawer spaces, they converted the cabinet into a shelf of pigeonholes and stowed the salvaged medicines away. Then they swept and dusted and, finally, opened the shutters.

Until sundown they sat there, talking of the Jewel, Master Crowe telling Duffy stories while they both kept their eyes on the door. But no customers came.

"Is there not one toothache in Elford Town?" Master Crowe wondered aloud. "Not a single bee sting?"

Duffy, as if joining in a game, added, "Nor burnt finger? Nor freckled maiden who wishes to be milk-fair?" But his jokes did not return a smile to Master Crowe's face.

Nor did Pajara return.

Iseult, though, appeared somewhat improved. Duffy changed the blackened poultice each time he turned the hourglass, and she ate two pigeon eggs Master Crowe found on the ledge outside the loft window. She still didn't move around much in her box, but she rubbed her face against Duffy's hand as a cat might.

Just at twilight, someone came at last: Harry Buck, the town crier, carrying a parchment, a hammer, and nails.

"Greetings, Harry," called Master Crowe. "Did that infusion clear away the twins' measles?"

Harry Buck's normally ruddy face went a shade redder. "Oh, aye, aye," he stammered.

"No deafness came of the illness, no blindness? The fever broke in time?"

"No . . . that is, aye, they're hale enow, up and about today. . . ." The man looked profoundly uncomfortable. At last he blurted out, "Magistrate sent me, sir, I shan't stay." So saying, he turned and, with a few blows of the hammer, fastened a parchment to the outside of the shop door. Then he turned back to face Master Crowe for a moment, as if debating whether to speak again.

"Something about the magistrate?" Master Crowe prodded quietly.

"Sir . . ." Harry stared at the hammer as if it had settled in his hand all unbidden and unfamiliar, like a strangely tame bird. "Master Crowe, sir, never have you done me harm, nor my wife nor children, neither. And often you've been help to us, well I know it. And I've paid you fair and quick, haven't I? It's true, there's no grudge betwixt you and me, is there?" He swallowed hard and hurriedly continued. "So you know I'm speaking as one who wishes you well, and not hold it against me if I tell you—you'd best get out of Elford, while you still can. There's bad feelings stirring all around, sir, has been for a while, but folks try to live and let live. And I'm not saying I blame you for Mistress Cotter's score. She deserves what she gets, I say. But this business of stealing the sun, and turning folks into toads and back again . . . Well, I'm your friend, as I say, and you'll not misconstrue me if I say, well, perhaps you should move out into the wilds, like. They say many magicians do. Elford's just too civilized for those kinds of goings-on, sir. You can see that now, sir, can't you?"

The crier's face, by this time, was the color of a boiled beet. He hastily pulled his forelock and backed out the door without even a good-bye.

In the silence that followed his exit, Duffy asked timidly, "What does the parchment say, Master?"

Moving slowly, Crowe walked across the shop, stepped outside, and read aloud the magistrate's decree. "*In the name of public safety, the shop of the Apothecary Crowe shall be closed henceforth and forever. Citizens, beware.*"

Chapter 17

A Fool's Decision

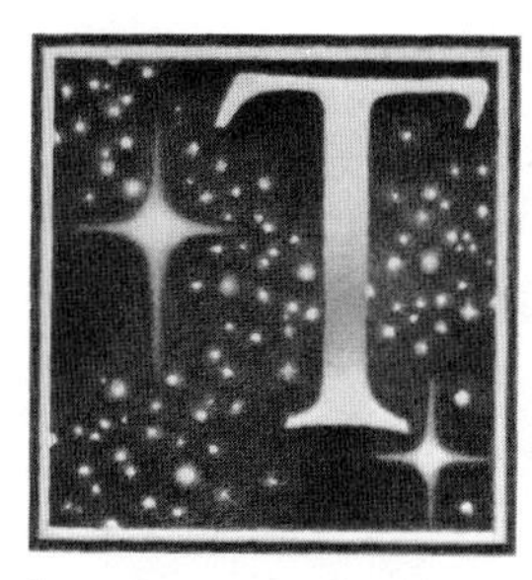

HE SHOP WAS VERY QUIET. THROUGH THE open door, the last blue glow of twilight cast deep shadows into the little square caves of the broken medicine cabinet. A bit of something was sticking up between two rough floorboards, and Duffy stopped to inspect it. It was a turquoise quill. Pajara must have lost it struggling out of George Tallow's sack.

The apothecary was the first to speak. "Harry's twins, Joan and Robin, must be just about your age, now. As much alike as sister and brother could be, a pretty pair. Harry is a fine father, too. When they had fever, he sat up with them as often as his wife Polly did." Crowe came slowly across the room. "He's a good man, Duffy."

"I don't care for him," Duffy said, his voice small and hard. "You saved his precious children for him and now he tells you to get out of town. 'Turning folks into toads and back again,' he said. George probably told them you really *did* it, I wager, and Harry *believed* it."

Master Crowe smiled wearily. "And didn't you, yourself, ask if I could do it?" Duffy blushed, but the old man waved a hand vaguely, as if to brush away any embarrassment. "I am fairly served, I imagine. I have not gone out of my way to explain to anyone the true extent and limit of my science. Being needed, I did not think much about being loved."

In the dim light, Crowe looked hardly more than a shadow. *How old he must be*, Duffy thought suddenly. Most old people lived with their grown sons or daughters. They sat in their sunny gardens with grandchildren playing around them. For the first time, it occurred to him that Crowe had no such family, no such home. He had nothing but his work—and his apprentice.

Then, in the slow swelling of his heart, Duffy thought: *Until I came here, I had nothing, either.*

He walked across the shop and awkwardly touched the apothecary's arm. There were so many words he had not had occasion to say.

"*I* love you, Master Crowe," he said.

Crowe looked at him steadily. "I know you do, Duffy. You did not wait for much testing of me. And I love you as well. So you see, it is easy for me to understand Harry. He loves his family, and even the chance that some danger might come to them through me is fearful to him. That is the way it is with everyone in Elford. They are frightened, and so they become mean. Harry riles up no anger in himself, at least."

"Mistress Cotter has no family!"

Crowe laughed a little. "She is still affrighted, maybe, for the one she loves best," he said. "How could she bear it if the face she saw in her looking glass were that of a toad?"

"Unless her glass lies, that's what she *does* see." Duffy was relieved to grin. As wit, it was feeble enough, but it made him feel less helpless.

Crowe smiled abstractedly, his thoughts working ahead. "We ought to consider our next move carefully."

He began pacing again, thinking out loud. "If they believe I can put out the sun, I could work some bargain with them, I suppose. Ask my price to bring it back. I have heard of sorcerers who have done such things." He laughed dryly. "Charlatans."

He walked over to the shop door, paused on the threshold, and regarded the magistrate's sign with a wry expression. " '*Public safety . . . Citizens beware.*' I tell you, Duffy, if magic gave you no power at all, you could still eat well on the ignorance of your neighbors. But, I like it not. Such thoughts are cowardly. Our art is one of truth. How could we hope to serve it with lies? I should not have dealt so deceitfully with George. Perhaps, after all, Harry's suggestion *is* best. If my calculations are correct, we have only three days. The eclipse will surely panic anyone who isn't already openly against us."

"But what would happen to the workroom, your tools, your books, your . . . ?"

"I suppose they'd be burned in my place, if folk became truly convinced of all this devil business." Master Crowe spoke almost lightly, but it was the first he had acknowledged to Duffy how genuinely dangerous their situation was becoming. "They'd not know the value of the things, nor trust them. I suppose that also means we cannot sell them nor pawn them here in Elford. To think," he suddenly exclaimed in frustration, "we made the Stone in this place! And I don't see how we can travel without at least a bit of coin. Oh, one or two towns, perhaps, we could get through. To Edgarsford or Cookstown, maybe as far as Smith's Crossing. We could walk *that* far. There's part of yesterday's loaf left, and the cheese. We could find enough berries and greens to keep our bellies full for a while. But if we did run, count on all Elford Town considering it ample proof of wrongdoing and spreading the word. We'd not be safe for long, wherever we stopped."

"But before anyone heard, couldn't we sell enough herbs to hire a cart to take us farther away?"

"Aye, we could do that, I imagine. Or perhaps Wing could lend us something. . . ."

Duffy could hear the doubt in his voice, and suddenly, urgently, he begged, "Master, can't we at least *try* to make some gold?"

A sad, tender look was in the old man's face. "Ah, Duffy, you *do* think like an alchemist. But you are so young. It may be years before we see the Stone again—if we *ever* do so. And whatever treasure we make from fear, we will not succeed in making anything while intending to escape our unsolved problem. Besides," he added practically, "if the golden sun is approaching eclipse, the odds against any increase in gold would be immense."

"Herbs, then," Duffy said flatly. "Or Master Wing."

"Truth to tell, child, none of these plans sets well with me." Master Crowe stopped to look out at the dark street. "True enough, there are times to run, times when only a fool would *not* run. . . ." He shook his head soberly. "There are also times to stand. Look you there, Duffy."

Duffy left the bench and came over by the old man to look out the window. Master Crowe continued to speak, his voice gentle, but urgent as Duffy's own had been a moment before.

"The sky is very black, is it not? Black and endless. If it weren't for the stars, surely the weight of the great darkness would stifle us. But there are the stars, pinning the sky up and making it beautiful as well."

Duffy nodded.

"Yet the stars are not pin-sized," Crowe went on, and Duffy realized there was fresh amazement in the old man's words. "They are only at such great distance, they seem small. The light is more distilled, more refined and intense than the darkness, so they are really equal in the scales of heaven. Were we close to the stars, they should not seem petty and cold, but enormous: spheres all aflame, glorious worlds."

Crowe rested his hand on Duffy's shoulder. "And look at Elford, this small, mean town that calls us names. 'Tis dark, even as the sky is. And it has stars—do you see them?"

"The windows?"

"Aye. And each speck of light we see from our window is not really a speck, but a whole, fire-lit room where folk eat soup, and play puss-in-the-corner with the children, and pet the dogs." Master Crowe sounded almost as if he were talking to himself, so low did he speak. "Anyone out alone at night is easy to frighten, for the night itself, throughout each and every life, remains strange and unknown. Magic and science are unknown to most folk, and dreadful as a dark night. *We* are terrible to them. And in turn, they are frightful to us, with their threats. But if we saw each other more closely, who can say? Would it not all appear great and warm as the stars? *As above, so below*—so the teachers have always maintained. We must always inquire of our own daily lives, or it makes no difference at all."

The look on Crowe's face at that moment was the one he had worn when the Stone blinked out, and Duffy wondered at it.

"I am reluctant to run, child. I want to stay, though it may prove to be a fool's decision. What say you, Duffy? What do *you* think?"

Duffy looked still at Master Crowe. "I guess we ought to stay." Yet as he looked out again at the winking lights, they might have been so many glaring eyes. He remembered the fear in Harry Buck's face, and the venom in Mistress Cotter's words. He thought for a second of Hugh and Bertie, but their faces blurred in his mind with George's. He wondered how a grey old man and an undersized boy could hope even to hold off the bad will of an entire town, much less turn it into friendship.

As if in answer to his misgivings, Master Crowe said, "Something will happen, Duffy. I feel it in my bones. Something will happen."

But Duffy could feel no cheer at that. *Of course something will happen,* he thought. *But will it be something good?*

Chapter 18

"Such Time as We Have . . ."

A T FIRST DUFFY HOPED THAT SOMEONE, ANY-one, would brave the magistrate's wrath and come to the shop. But in the two days that followed, it soon became apparent that it was not just the magistrate who was keeping people away. The stories and rumors were doing their work as well.

Duffy and Crowe sat in the shop alone, from dawn to dusk, and spoke to no one but each other. Not daring to go out into the town, they ate only the food they had on hand, making do without fresh milk, without Mistress Wheat's brown bread.

It was a tense, tedious time, which Master Crowe filled as best he could by teaching Duffy more herb lore and recounting tales of his own youth and travels.

And there were more of the magical tales, too, stories as strangely colored as dreams, filled with dark jewels and bright animals, and kingdoms where the laws were not decrees set down on parchment, but vines that grew and flowered. These were the stories Duffy liked best, and when Crowe made up riddles based on them, Duffy's answers were sometimes better than his master's, delighting them both.

Though they watched for her continually, Pajara did not return. Crowe tended Iseult's wound and kept it cleansed, and Duffy fed her soppets of bread and broth. Her pain seemed to lessen and she was beginning to mend. As she recovered strength, she learned to hold her chin up to get her throat stroked.

"'Tis odd she turned so white," Duffy remarked idly as he fed her supper. Iseult's coat had indeed paled as though touched by frost.

"Do you not know why?" Crowe asked, smiling. "She has had her royal battle, and now she becomes a royal beast. She is an ermine now."

"I am glad I changed her name, then," Duffy said. Hiding a sly grin, he added, regarding the old man's white hair and beard, "You never told me *you* were in a battle, Master."

The old man's expression was puzzled for a moment. Then he shouted with laughter. "Only one, my boy: the Fools' Campaign against Ignorance! But sometimes that seems a campaign that's been raging forever." He shook his white head. "No, no, I have always been a scholar; I did not go to the wars. How would I have hewn at men with one hand and healed them with the other?" His face grew sober. "But who knows what battles may come here to us in our own home?"

Duffy's eyes registered shock, and Crowe rushed on, trying with all his strength to put words together to carry Duffy beyond this grim thought. "But I pray *you* may be spared. No, no interruption, my boy, hear me out. Your very dreams know all the ancient rules of alchemy. You were born with magic in you. Do you not know that these guessing games we have played at these last few days are great mysteries? How often have I heard you guess riddles that would bow a wise man's head? Your first attempt at alchemy brought forth the Jewel. I have been thinking long on this. Long. Tomorrow you must go away."

Duffy looked puzzled.

"Child, my child." Crowe groaned as he watched Duffy's bewildered face. "I make you old too soon. But what can I do? We have a tradition to carry on. How can we pray to be preserved ourselves, except by giving ourselves over to preserving truth? Such time as we still have, I will use to teach you as much as possible. If the town should rise against me, nothing will be left of our tools and books. The stories are all I may bequeath to you, Duffy. Learn them. Love them well."

Duffy stared at his master. He did not know what to say. An apprentice, when all was said and done, must obey. Duffy knew he could not argue now, so was silent. But he knew there were tears behind his eyes.

Crowe shook his head sorrowfully. He took Duffy's hand and gently led him up the stairway onto the roof of the shop. There they gazed silently at the strew of stars.

"There is no moon tonight," Crowe said at last. "From my calculations I know that Elford will see the sun disappear tomorrow."

Then Duffy put his arms around the old man, and Crowe hugged him close. Though Duffy's face was hidden in the folds of the threadbare gown, and his heart was pounding in his ears, he could not cry.

Chapter 19

Night at Noon

Both Duffy and Master Crowe were up before dawn the next day. Surprisingly, neither of them had slept badly that night. It was as if their tense, overwrought bodies knew they must be well rested in order to deal with whatever was to come.

Before first light, they crept out of the back door and down to the river, their backs bent under yokes and buckets, for the cistern was low.

"And there are many emergencies that demand a good supply of water," Master Crowe had said.

It was the first they had ventured out since the shop had been closed, and though no one seemed to be about at that hour except themselves, Duffy felt some trepidation. They made three trips, with Crowe carrying four buckets each time and Duffy two. As they turned back toward home the last time, the river was just starting to run rosy with dawn, and they heard the cocks in Feather Lane.

Duffy paused, head to one side. He had not forgotten the chilling trumpet of the cockatrice, and he wondered if sunup would always remind him of that other world's hot wind and Iseult's saving courage.

"Now," Crowe was saying, "I have written a note for you to take to Wing. He will see to your care. Perhaps there will be no—" Suddenly, the old man staggered. One of the buckets on his yoke knocked against the wall at his side, and water splattered out.

Duffy threw off his own yoke and went immediately to his master.

Crowe's face was grey, but he began to speak again. "Perhaps there will be no trouble . . . and then you can come back."

"Master, you are ill."

"No, no, child, I am only old." But Crowe let Duffy lift the heavy yoke off his shoulders, leaning on him as they walked back to their own wicket.

By the time Duffy had fetched in the last buckets of water, his mind was set.

"There is the message for Wing," Crowe said gently from the pallet where he rested. He pointed toward a paper on the workbench.

"I am not going," said Duffy.

"You must go. It may not be safe here."

"You signed my papers," Duffy countered desperately. "You can't send away an apprentice without reason. Master, don't make me go. What if you *are* ill? And perhaps there will be no trouble. You said so yourself. Let me stay with you."

Crowe looked slowly around the workroom, at the shelves of musty books, the cobwebbed corners—at the jar that held the snake, and the one that held the remainder of the magical feather. Dust was already settled on them.

He looked at Duffy. Most boys his age had families—fathers to sing to them, mothers to watch after them. Most boys his age were still playing with tops and hoops, with wooden swords.

Crowe passed his right hand across his eyes. His left arm felt a bit numb. "Stay with me, then."

They had not opened the shop's front door since Harry Buck's visit, but had been keeping it barred and locked, and the shutters as well. With a great deal of pushing and pulling, Duffy got the herb cabinet over against one window, and a high-backed chair against the other, as additional barriers. The door was heavy oak with stout iron hinges, and less likely to be broken. However crazed or angry, a mob would have a hard time getting at them.

The back wicket was more of a problem. The passage from the workroom was high-vaulted, but it was narrow, and there was no piece of furniture just the right size to wedge across it as a blockade.

"Besides," Crowe told Duffy, "despite my weakness, we may have to attempt a hasty flight after all. The alley, with the river at one end and all the smaller alleyways branching off it toward other parts of town, will be our best chance. Remember."

Duffy nodded and merely locked the grilled gate, pulling a counter across the inner archway of the passage. He realized that, attacked from that side, they would be trapped like mice, with only the stairs to the roof for exit. But it was the best he could devise.

"For want of any better pastime, then," as Crowe put it, they mixed a tincture of foxglove. "A useful tonic," the old man muttered. "Dangerous but useful."

The sun climbed higher in the sky, burning its way through the summer blue as if it were any ordinary summer sun, any normal day.

It was a little before eleven o'clock when the barking started. Duffy recognized the nervous baying of Will Coxy's old blind bloodhound, Caesar, because there were no other bloodhounds this end of Elford. Then another puzzled bark joined in, from over on the north side of the market. Then two or three of the gravel-throated bullterriers from the butcher's quarter added their noise. In a minute, the whole town was chaotic with the yippings, whinings, and growlings of a hundred beasts.

Duffy knew that animals were often the first to sense something strange about to happen. Nor was it only the dogs making the commotion. Horses were neighing uneasily, donkeys braying, hens cackling.

Then a new sound began as housewives scolded their noisy pets, and drivers cursed their suddenly uncontrollable beasts.

Duffy climbed onto the chair by the shop window and peeked out through a crack in the shutter. The street outside was all in a pother. A hissing tomcat shied from a cart horse. The horse, backing suddenly, tangled his traces and trampled the foot of the carter's helper. The carter's helper stumbled sideways and knocked over a milkmaid, pails and all, and the girl loudly bewailed her misfortune to anyone who would listen.

Just then, Mistress Cotter turned into the street, mincing along with the self-important air of a fashionable lady and holding up her skirts so her red slippers showed. Every few steps, however, she had to pause and tug at her puppy's leash, coaxing in a honeyed voice.

"Come, precious, come like a good doggie. No, no, mustn't cry so, come ahead, no, *no, mustn't* tangle one's skirts, oh, *do* stop that noise, one's nerves are *so* delicate. . . ."

The spaniel ignored his mistress's entreaties and howled like any common hound, the hair along his neck standing up like a brush. Then he saw the spilled milk puddled on the cobbles and darted forward to lap up the mess. Since his leash was still tangled around Mistress Cotter's daintily shod feet, his sudden movement dragged her into the midst of the weeping, cursing, hissing group of cat, horse, driver, helper, and milkmaid. Her red shoes a milk-sodden ruin, Mistress Cotter added her own curses to the clamor, and she no longer bothered to maintain a gentlewoman's soft tones.

The blue of the sky suddenly seemed to deepen a shade, almost as if a cloud had passed before the sun. But there were no clouds in the sky. The angry people in the street did not take immediate notice, but Duffy, watching through the shutter, saw the change and called urgently to Master Crowe.

"Master, something is happening in the sky."

The shadows outside were of unusual sharpness, and the colors everywhere—the carter's orange shirt, the heap of green cabbages in his cart, Mistress Cotter's scarlet gown—took on a twilight glow that shone eerily at midday.

The cat was the first to act on the change, and, with a screech, he bounded away as if the devil were after him. Then the horse stopped struggling with his harness and stood trembling, gazing toward the sky. One by one, the carter, his boy, the milkmaid, and finally Mistress Cotter sensed that something was amiss and fell silent, looking at each other in puzzlement.

Growling uncertainly, the spaniel gave a suspicious sniff at the cobblestones, then trotted over toward the closed door of the apothecary shop.

Duffy watched, unmoving, as the dog approached. He knew what would happen next, and there was nothing he could do to forestall it. Just then, Crowe joined him at the window.

The dog reached the threshold and evidently remembered his unpleasant experiences within the shop. His growls abruptly broke into a tirade of high-pitched barking.

Mistress Cotter turned, then, and stared at the shuttered windows. She could not have seen Duffy and Crowe watching from within, but she seemed to be looking at the exact spot where they stood. Her face contorted and her words cut through the noisy yammerings of her pet.

" 'Tis the old man," she cried. "Crowe! He's putting a curse on us for coming near his shop."

Duffy watched in horror, and yet in a kind of fascination, as the veil of fear dropped itself over her homely features.

'Tis almost as if she is talking herself into being afraid, he thought.

What had just a moment ago been nothing more than irritation over a pair of ruined shoes was now turning into an unshakable conviction that sorcery was at hand. In that long moment, Duffy wondered if, even had there been no eclipse, Mistress Cotter might eventually have convinced herself and others that Master Crowe could work evil spells.

But it was growing darker by the second. Now, for the first time, one of the group chanced to look upward. The milkmaid gasped, her hand rising involuntarily to her throat. She screamed.

"The sun! The sun is disappearing!"

Since the sun was nearly overhead, Duffy could not see it through the crack in the shutter. He could only watch the terrified expressions seizing the crowd. The carter's face hung slack, his mouth agape, his eyes bulging. His helper was blubbering. The girl had thrown her apron up over her head to hide from the sight, but she kept stealing glances from under the cloth every few seconds anyway, her eyes drawn back again and again to the impossible spectacle.

From all over Elford, groans and wails could be heard as people beheld the unspeakable miracle of the sun's shrinking.

In the dim light, Mistress Cotter looked like a madwoman. Her face was twisted and tense as a gargoyle on a church eave. Her eyes stretched open so wide, Duffy was certain he could make out white all around the dark center. Her lips were drawn back from her teeth like an animal's. She was wailing louder than the rest.

"It's the sorcerer. He said his demons would swallow the sun, and now they're doing it. He'll kill us all. Get Crowe! He's the one behind all this."

Dismayed murmurs ran through the gathering crowd.

"Crowe, the sorcerer?" shouted the carter, smacking one fist against the palm of his other hand. "He used magic on Lum's lame nag so it beat my grey mare in the races last Saint Dunstan's fair. He's the one to blame, all right."

"The sorcerer!"

"The wizard!"

"Get Crowe! If we want the sun back, we'll have to get the old heathen."

"Call the magistrate! Call out the guard!"

In the streets of Elford, people were running everywhere, shouting and screaming. It had grown almost as dark as night and many had taken up torches. The only ones not crying out, it seemed, were the two who watched from behind the shutter of the apothecary shop.

"What are they doing, Master?" Duffy asked, slipping his hand into the old man's.

"I don't know, child," Crowe replied, unwilling even now to expose Duffy to the worst of his own fears. He knew a person convicted of sorcery might be gaoled, or he might be hanged. Some were even burned at the stake.

"Duffy," Master Crowe said, "I think it best that you head for the river, out the back way. I cannot let them see you with me. They might harm you."

Duffy looked out at the firelit faces in the street and thought longingly of the river passing gently, even then, between grassy banks toward the sea. "Yes, let's go. There ought to be an old rowboat down by the landing, and no one will be there now."

Master Crowe interrupted softly. "I cannot go with you, lad. The tincture we mixed, the foxglove . . . is for me. My heart is old." He fluttered a hand wryly. "I am too slow a traveler now. Indeed, I am no traveler at all. It would be gambling with your life; it would be taking my own."

Duffy's expression stayed blank and Crowe forced himself to explain further. "Their fear holds them yet, but not long. You must go. *Now.*"

Still Duffy said nothing, but his mouth was set.

Master Crowe put coaxing into his voice, like honey in a bitter tea. "If it comes to nothing at all, I will send for you and bring you back to care for me and work with me. Most likely that is what shall happen, so you needn't feel badly about going, Duffy. Only do be quick, before some of these dunces start into the back alley and cut you off."

His voice was light, but Duffy was not fooled.

"No," said Duffy. "I will not go. When the magistrate comes, Mistress Cotter is going to be telling stupid lies about what you said in the shop the day she barged in. She's out there telling everyone right now that she saw you talking to the devil. I am your apprentice. *And* I am your only witness. I'll tell the magistrate she's lying, and they won't dare hurt you. Then when the sun comes back, everything will be fine."

Master Crowe shook his head. "Duffy, you won't be able to talk sense with them. They won't listen to you any more than to me. If you—"

His words were interrupted by a dull *whump* as something hit the outside of the door. There was another impact and then another. The mob was beginning to throw things.

When Duffy cautiously peered out through the shutter again, he saw they were tossing broken cobblestones, filth from the gutter, cabbages from the protesting farmer's cart.

And then, someone deep in the milling crowd threw a lighted torch.

The torch arched over the heads of the mob, an angry wad of illumination, and landed by the front wall. For long seconds, it didn't seem as if the wall could catch, old and dry though the timbers were, for the flame was not directly against the wood. But a man came running up with an armload of straw and strewed it along the foundation of the building. It was ablaze in a moment, and the shop walls with it.

CHAPTER 20

THE FIRE AND THE STARS

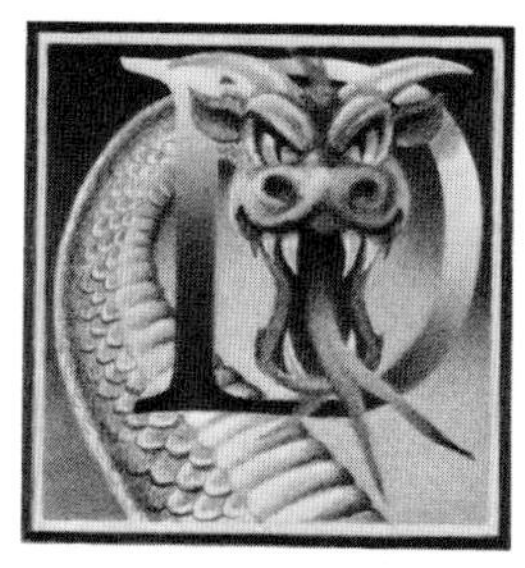

UFFY WAS DOWN THE STAIRS IN A MOMENT and back again with a bucket of water. There were no flames inside the shop yet, but smoke was seeping through the cracks in the wall, and, combined with the darkness outside, it made vision extremely difficult. The air was hot and thick as he doused the walls with water, hoping to wet them enough to keep the fire from spreading.

But outside, the crowd was bringing more straw to heap against the door and boarded windows.

Through the growing roar of the flames, he heard a man's voice shouting, "Get some men around back or the magician will get away."

So the alley was to be blocked. There would be no escape to the river after all.

Soon one of the weaker shutter boards charred through, and then the fire was inside the shop, as well as outside. Duffy ran down to the cellar again, sprung the door on Iseult's tin box, and set it on the floor near the rear door passage.

Back up the stairs carrying water, he saw Master Crowe trying to snuff the outbreak with an old piece of rug. But it seemed an uneven contest. The room was filled with smoke, and runners of flickering scarlet were creeping all around the shop.

Then, as Duffy ran toward the stairs for the last of the water left in the cistern, a bit of fire clutched at his own jerkin's ragged hem. By the time he was in the cellar, he felt the searing heat on his back. He was on fire!

At first, in his panic, Duffy ran across the room, trying to tear off his burning clothing. The running only fanned the flame. So he threw himself down on the floor and finally put out the fire by rolling on it.

But as he rolled, he knocked over a small cupboard and shattered a glass jar—the jar that held the cockatrice feather.

The magical feather, the feather of so much use to the alchemist, fluttered to the rush-covered floor. And the rushes, which had only smoldered a little from the burning jerkin, now burst into tongues of purple and gold flame where the feather lay.

Strong-scented curls of smoke billowed up and began to permeate the room, and, lying on the floor, Duffy saw it and thought: *Oh, no! not again, not now!*

The room was already wavering and blanking out in silver clouds. He fought to keep his eyes open, to get to his feet. But even as he rose, the twisting haze began to grow spumy, then solidified into strange walls of rough stone, dim and towering, with here and there a pillar of damp rock. Suddenly he was in a tunnel so high that the roof was invisible in shadow.

He began to run, his mind in turmoil. He could think of nothing clearly, but he knew Master Crowe was trapped in the burning apothecary shop, ill, helpless, surrounded by people who would do nothing to save him. Iseult, who'd saved his life, might not have the strength now to find her own way out of danger. And here *he* was, worlds away, where he could do nothing, where he could see nothing but the long, dim hallways through which he ran. He did not even try to keep track of the turns he made in the endless underground maze of passages.

Maybe the sun will come back soon, and the people of Elford will see that everything is all right, and feel ashamed of themselves for being so quick to blame. Then Master Crowe will be safe, he thought.

But Duffy had no idea how long the sun might stay hidden. He could only run on and on, hoping to get to some help. When he could run no farther, he pressed a hand against his aching side and walked.

After a while, a speck of light appeared at the end of the tunnel.

"At last," he murmured. "At least I will be out of the ground soon."

But presently, as he continued to walk, he realized the light did not mean the end of the tunnel, for it had not the brightness of day, nor even of moonlight, but was rather a dark, tight red. Gradually, he even began to feel warm, and the air became smoky, just as if he were approaching a raging furnace.

Could it be the burning apothecary shop? he wondered. *Am I really almost home? Will I be in time to help Master Crowe? Can I keep Iseult from disappearing in the confusion?*

Taking a halting breath, hand still clutched to his side, he sped up again, toward that light.

When he came to it, he sobbed in horror. Instead of the little shop, he stood looking into a cavern, illuminated a dirty scarlet and littered everywhere: littered with the glitter of gold and silver, heaps and mountains of smoldering jewels, a rainbow of brooding color. The treasure had been scooped into a nest, sloping down from near the ceiling to a wide hollow in the center of the cave. And lying in the hollow, bathed in the ruddy light of its own breath, was an immense, horned dragon.

Its eyes were tiny and green and looked like wet silk. A split tongue flicked in and out of its mouth. Its nostrils opened, red and angry.

But it was not the sight of the dragon, nor yet the fumes of acrid breath, that drained away all of Duffy's hope. For as he watched the swell and measure of its scaled, blue-black sides, he saw beyond doubt that he could not escape it. It was neither a sleeping snake nor a proud, new-hatched monstrosity. Duffy knew that he had fallen into the very marrow of the earth, into the keep of the most ancient, most subtle serpent of all: a creature that could never die.

And he knew more than that. He knew how this beast lived, how it watched. Should he turn to flee, he knew before and beyond all learning that the green eyes would spy him out immediately.

Yet there was no way he could cross the cavern to the other side where the tunnel opened again. He would be torn apart before he could go four steps. He knew all this without knowing how he knew. But he knew it perfectly.

The dragon heaved its glinting blue-black carcass to its feet and began dragging its weight back and forth, slavering, and hissing—a sound like wind against rusty metal.

Duffy's knees had no strength in them. *I am done for,* he thought. He didn't even wish for a sword, because a sword would have been useless. The dragon filled his heart with helpless horror. *This must be the end of all,* his reason told him.

Homing in on Duffy's scent, the dragon lumbered closer. Its great finned tail thrashed around, slamming against the stone walls, and sending showers of gold and silver flying each time it scraped across the floor. And not only gold and silver, for its own steely blue scales caught on the rock, ripped off, and rattled down around Duffy, a grisly rain.

Then for one trembling second the dragon was still. Its tongue flickered out hungrily as it looked directly into Duffy's eyes.

In that moment, Duffy thought: *I wonder if it will chew me up or just swallow me whole?*

He felt anger wash through his body, and a hatred so bitter it left his mind far behind. He was suddenly sharply aware of his own teeth and nails and muscles, as if they were all the weapons he needed, and of his spine drawing itself together as if he could himself strike like a serpent.

Again the dragon hissed, and again there was a spatter of gold and blue-black hail.

And Duffy the apprentice remembered suddenly: stars that fell around a dancing figure. Remembered: harmony. No more monstrous hiss, no grunting beast. He remembered Crowe teaching him "*the song of the stars. . . .*" The thought lasted for only a tithe of a second, but it was enough.

"You shall not have me," Duffy said softly. He would not be caught, because Master Crowe could not put out the fire by himself, and even because Elford Town needed Master Crowe. Besides, who would care for Iseult? Who would find Pajara? Who would learn of herbs and alchemy?

I will not be caught! It was as if his strength were becoming more than one boy's strength, his courage more than one boy's courage; so that when the horned head of the dragon thrust up close and opened its vast mouth to roar and swallow, Duffy thought faster than the forked tongue could flicker. His hands grabbed the horns on the dragon's brow and, desperately, he hoisted himself up.

The black tongue shot out just beneath Duffy's dangling feet, wet and glistening with poison, but Duffy didn't see it. The moment he'd touched the dragon's horns, something new had happened.

The cave walls had melted and flowed away, and a shimmering river of starlight was splashing cool drops against his hot forehead. Rainbows opened around him, flowerlike; the sky flushed with the good smell of moss and old earth. His hands were cool and strong and curled around the two ivory arms of the great moon, and he was grown great himself so that he flew amongst the sky, laughing for joy.

Then a wizened voice from deep in the pit of his stomach whimpered.

Duffy, you are all alone in the sky!
Duffy, you are too high up and you will fall!
You are only a child, and those are real stars!
Let go! You can't hold on! LET GO!

Duffy's left hand slipped and lost its hold.

The dragon was all aflame below him with colors like rotting wood. The great finned tail churned the rainbow mists into dripping froth. Stars rained down like golden tears all around, until Duffy thought there'd soon be none left at all. And the poison tongue snapped out, slapping toward Duffy's feet.

I'm too small, he thought. *I need help.* His right hand started to slip.

The dragon's jaws quivered, strained, and blood and venom spilled out like dead oceans while the monster's roars rose to a tempest. The tongue shot toward a spinning star.

But then, in the center of it all, a still, calm voice inside Duffy's heart said simply: *No demon can swallow a star.*

"You cannot do that," Duffy called, and his left hand went up, up, and grabbed the dragon's horn once more.

The ivory moon spun out like music and cast Duffy free, and he flew and floated for seconds and moments and for an eternity, and landed in the tunnel on the other side of the cavern. At his feet lay a silver ring with a jewel large as a lark's egg and clear as springwater: clear, with a blood-red heart. Duffy picked it up, put it on his hand, and walked on.

Chapter 21

Elford Town

In the sky over Elford Town there was no sun. Man and beast alike looked up and shuddered to see the ring of fire that hung at the zenith. Though the clock in the church tower was striking noon, the sky was black as midnight.

A stranger came up to the edge of the crowd gathered in front of the apothecary shop. It was high summer, but he wore a long cloak with a hood that almost hid his face. He gazed at the inferno in astonishment and demanded, "Why is there no water line?" When no one answered, he grabbed the arm of the man nearest to him. "Why do you stand like ninnies while the shop burns? Come on, we can put it out yet, if we look sharp."

"Can't you see what's happening?" the local man retorted, pointing up at the sky. "The old man who owns the shop is a sorcerer. Why do you think the sun vanished? Because Crowe had his demons steal it, that's why. Told us all he'd do it."

An oath of disbelief leapt from the foreigner's tongue. "Are you a fool?" he cried. "Is this a town of fools?"

"'Tis the only way to be rid of the old devil," another man chimed in nervously, "so I'd mind me manners if I was—"

"He's in there still?" The man in the hood stared at the horrifying spectacle. Smoke and flame were pouring upward from the wooden building, blotting out the eerie twinkling of noonday stars. With a single motion, he cast off his billowing cloak.

"The vagabond—the old man's crony!" screeched Mistress Cotter. "He's in on it, too."

But few were listening, for the man had leapt toward the fire. Seizing a heavy piece of wood that lay nearby, he battered at the charred shutter while sparks flew into his hair and stung his face. It hardly seemed possible that a man could tolerate such ferocious heat. But when the shutter gave way, he hoisted himself across the sill and disappeared inside.

To Djano's smoke-wrung eyes, the shop did indeed seem hellish, the unnatural thickness of the air stabbed by trails of flame and flying sparks. In the far corner of the room, almost invisible in the pall, was the apothecary, his face sooty and his long beard singed. He was feebly swinging a steaming rag of carpet, smothering one nest of fire, only to see another spring to life inches away.

"Djano, son of Alonzo," he greeted the newcomer, a faint, grim smile on his lips. "You choose an ill-omened time to visit."

"Keep close to the floor, Master—the smoke is thinner there. Is your boy safe?"

"He went to fetch water and has not come back. He may be trapped. I fear to let this get out of hand lest the floor collapse into the cellar."

"Can you manage here a bit longer?"

Crowe's expression was oddly distant, but he nodded. Djano bounded down the stairs to the workroom.

There was no fire in the cellar, and the smoke was not as dense as upstairs. The cistern stood open, and the bucket lay empty on the floor next to it. Djano checked the back gate where he had entered a few days before. It was locked and barricaded. The apprentice was nowhere to be seen. Dipping up the last of the water, Djano ran back upstairs.

The old man now lay crumpled in the corner. His lungs raw and rebellious in the brooding atmosphere, Djano lifted the frail form and struggled with it, out over the sill and into the midday darkness of Elford Town.

The crowd fell suddenly silent as they watched Djano approach. Was the old man still alive? Was the stranger a sorcerer himself?

A joist must have burned through just then, for a slew of sparks erupted from the shop roof, and the watching townsfolk gasped with one voice. Then a handful of cockleshells rattled on the cobbles, and one hit the stranger's knee. The boys from Fish Lane were not easily cowed.

Mistress Cotter licked a drop of spittle from the corner of her thin lips. The fire had not gotten rid of the old man, and the sky above was as black as the Styx. In the heat of the burning shop, she imagined she felt the devil's wrath gathering. She feared, finally, where that wrath would actually fall first. Terror clutched at her stringy throat, and she cried into the ungodly hush.

"Stones! It's them or us! Stone the sorcerers!"

The vagabond did not even look in her direction, but set down the old man with great tenderness. He did not seem to raise his voice, yet the words carried all the way to the edge of the crowd. "Someone bring me some water. He's not dead yet."

"Get them while you have the chance!" Mistress Cotter's voice had not been sweet to begin with, and now it hardly sounded like a woman's.

"Who will bring water? Quickly!"

"Stone the sorcerer!" She herself took up a stick but hesitated still, a moment, to fling it.

"Water! He will die!"

The crowd seemed to waver like the smoke that hung in the air. Then, with a sob, Harry Buck broke away and ran toward the river. Yet most of the townsfolk kept their distance, and shopkeepers, farm wives, clerks, and footmen murmured uneasily about the Evil Eye until Harry Buck returned. Mistress Cotter's screams were dwindling to babble; she tugged at sleeves, gesturing fearfully.

At last, outraged, Djano would hear no more. Relinquishing the unconscious Crowe to Harry Buck and the fresh water, Djano pushed through the crowd until he stood within arm's length of Mistress Cotter. She shrank from him and fell silent, fear in her eyes.

"You," he ordered her, in his powerful player's voice, "use your head instead of your spiteful tongue. If Crowe were a magician, as you say, would he be lying there now close to death? If he were hell's minion, could fire harm him?" He turned to the crowd. "Is there no one among you who knows science and history? Are you all so ignorant as this creature? It was not by magic that the sun was dimmed, nor will it be magic that brings it back."

His words carried the weight of many years of public eloquence, but a fishwife shouted scornfully, "Where is it gone, then? If everyone in *your* country is so wise, tell us *that*."

"It has gone nowhere!" Djano said clearly. "It is between the spheres of heaven and will make itself visible again soon enough for you to see by its light what fools you have for neighbors. I have traveled in many lands, I tell you. I saw this same thing happen twelve years ago in India. The sun will come back, I say."

"What proof is that?" cried Mistress Cotter. "Everyone knows that India is full of heathen magicians."

"Heathen, is it?" sniffed Harry Buck's wife, Polly. She was a solid, stout woman and her tone was blessedly matter-of-fact as it fell on the crowd. "Master Crowe is no more heathen nor I am, Drusilla Cotter."

"Seems like he couldn't be," the milkmaid added doubtfully. "He cured my sister's babe of the fever afore we had the little thing christened. I don't think as the devil would like being cheated like that, you know."

A housewife nodded. "And he cured my Neddy of a liver attack and told him not to drink so much wine, and Neddy took a right good scare from it and stopped carrying on so much. That weren't devil's work."

As the housewife finished her account, Djano felt a hesitant tug on his elbow and looked down to find a ragged boy standing there.

"Please, sir, the crier says the old man is not waking," said Bertie, "and he may be dying, and . . . and . . . please, sir, where is Duffy the 'prentice?" The whole crowd heard the child's voice.

Djano looked back at Mistress Cotter, his face pale. "May God show you kinder judgment than you have shown others," he said shortly. Without a glance backward, he strode toward the burning apothecary shop once more.

When he was still yards away, though, there was a roar and a mighty eruption of sparks from inside: the floor had given way and gone crashing into the cellar.

Chapter 22

The Jewel of Life

A cock crowed in Feather Lane, but the silent crowd did not notice.

The sky began to grow light. The wheel of fire filled with light, and for the second time that day, dawn came. This time, it did not rise from the earth's edge, but spilled down gently from the sky. Yet the people of Elford Town stared not at the heavens, but at the burning apothecary shop. Somehow it looked smaller in the growing daylight than it had in the darkness. Ashes smeared the teary faces of Hugh and Bertie, the almshouse boys.

Suddenly the shop door burst open. A plume of opal smoke rolled out, lit by the flames behind. Through the flames walked a blond boy. With his right hand, Duffy held Iseult the ermine safe against his shirt. On his left hand was a ring such as no one in the crowd had ever seen.

Duffy walked through the crowd as if he hardly knew it to be there and went straight to the spot where Harry Buck and his daughter Joan knelt over the still form of Master Crowe. Kneeling himself, Duffy gazed at the old man's face. Then, ever so gently, he touched the ring to his master's forehead.

The lines on Crowe's brow tensed momentarily, and then his

eyes opened. He smiled faintly up at Duffy. "I had such a clear dream," he murmured. "I was in a cavern, watching. . . ." Duffy grinned shyly. "You are a good boy, Duffy. A good apprentice. Where is the elixir?"

Duffy smiled and pulled the vial of foxglove from his pocket. "I brought it with me in case you should need it, Master." He poured a few drops between the old man's lips, whispering, "*For the Red Bird and the White are the Soul and the Spirit, but the Black Bird is the Body, which dwelleth on the Earth, and that Bird shall also fly.*"

Djano had pushed through the crowd by now and, with Harry Buck, helped Crowe to sit up and sip a little water.

The townsfolk looked up at the growing light, but for the most part they did not look at one another. One by one they drifted away, back to their homes and shops and errands. Several neighbors began to bring water to quench the dwindling flames of the ruined apothecary shop. No one noticed when Mistress Cotter sidled away, although quite a few noticed her spaniel nipping in and out around their feet, with George Tallow shamefacedly chasing after.

Djano whistled once, a low warbling call, and in a flutter of feathers, a small bird separated herself from the newly blue sky and settled on Duffy's shoulder.

"Pajara," Duffy cried out, "you've returned!"

Djano beamed with pride. "It was she who brought me back in the first place. I was in Wing's room when the ape began to gibber at something outside the window. Pajara was on the ledge. I knew there must be trouble or she would never be loose. So I left my Nania with Master Wing and came to repay your kindness, if I could. My Nania, she does not cough now."

"We are more than gladdened, seeing you. How greatly we are in *your* debt, now." Crowe's hand lay on Djano's tattered sleeve.

But Master Crowe did not look quite so glad when his glance went past Djano to the smoldering ruin of the shop. "So many precious instruments, so many books, lost forever," he murmured. "It will take years to sell enough medicines to replace those scholarly treasures, even if I bring myself to charge everyone full price." He sighed, gazing at the chimney. "The poor storks will have to build another nest."

Duffy looked, too. All that remained of the old place was the chimney and the embers of the great nest that had once so cheered him. The storks were circling overhead, as if themselves reluctant to believe in this misfortune.

Slowly, shyly, Duffy held out his hand, and the ring glittered in the sun. "Master, perhaps you could sell this and build another shop."

Master Crowe looked for the first time at the ring, and suddenly there were tears in his old eyes. "The Jewel, Duffy. Here with us, after all." His voice trembled with awe, as it never trembled with age. "And look, it is set in Philosophers' Silver, the stage the metal grows through last, before it becomes True Gold. But it's yours, child, your courage earned it, you should keep it. . . ."

"It is not yet True Gold, though, Master. If I am to be Duffy 'Prentice of Elford Town, I will need a shop here to serve in, won't I?"

On Duffy's shoulder, Pajara preened her emerald feathers, then swiveled her head to peer up at the bright blue sky.

"O, the sun, the sun," she chirped. "*Dia bellissima!*"